MW01537515

Copyright © 2016 Jessica Ashe

ROYALLY SCREWED is a work of fiction. Names, characters, places, and incidents are either the product of the author's imagination or are used fictitiously. Any resemblance to actual persons or their likeness is entirely coincidental.

This book contains mature content, including graphic sex scenes and adult language. Please do not continue reading if you are under the age of 18 or if this content is likely to offend you.

All characters in the book are 18+ years of age, not blood related, and all sexual acts are consensual.

All Rights Reserved.

ROYALLY SCREWED

By JESSICA ASHE

Chapter One

GEORGE

The only thing hurting worse than my head was my neck.

I tried to sit up, but my left arm was numb and wouldn't move from the bed.

The sun shone brightly through cheap curtains, blinding me and sending pain shooting through my head in the process. I recognized the nasty blue fabric covering the windows. I was in student halls again.

I looked down and saw the reason for my numb left arm and bad neck.

"Hey, sexy," a petite young blonde said, with the sweet innocence that only eighteen-year-olds could pull off. She was lying on my left arm, although to be fair she didn't have a lot of choice. Why did universities insist on putting single beds in student dorms? It was rather inconsiderate to those of us who like to screw students and then get a good night's sleep after.

Despite the headache, her perky tits captured my attention immediately, just as they had done last night in the bar. They weren't huge, but they were tender and her tiny, pale brown nipples had my mouth watering. She'd had them on display last night; I'd always been a sucker for a pert set of titties.

I winced as I pulled my arm out from under her neck, while trying to remain perched on the edge of the tiny bed. Not an easy feat for a guy of my size, although at least she didn't need a lot of room.

"Hey, gorgeous," I replied with a smile. At least we weren't using names, because I sure as shit didn't know hers.

Now I just needed to extricate myself from this situation without leaving behind a trail of tears. I never used to care how I left things, but now I had to worry about my reputation.

The news will be out in two weeks. Maybe less. We're just fact checking now. I hope you're ready.

That email still haunted me in my sleep. At least the journalist had given me a head's up. That was decent of her. She didn't have to do that, but I'd left her with pleasant memories from the night we'd spent together. See, it paid to sleep around; it was my way of developing contacts.

Knowing in advance didn't help much though. I just had two more weeks of freedom before 'my life got flipped—turned upside down' Fresh Prince style.

"What do you study?" she asked. Just those few words helped me pinpoint her as probably being local to Yorkshire. Or perhaps Manchester. Two years of living in York after moving up from Berkshire, and I still couldn't distinguish northern accents. I could identify people from Liverpool, Hull, and Newcastle, but everything else tended to mesh into one. I was a typical southern fairy in that regard.

"I'm not a student," I replied.

And thank God for that. Students were fun for fucking, but I couldn't bear to be around them for more than five minutes of conversation. They were either frustratingly full of ambition, or just flat-out pretentious.

Fortunately, the females of the species liked to let their hair down in the evenings. Hair down, and legs open: just how I liked them.

"I need to be in class in an hour," the blonde said, as her fingers tickled my chest. "That leaves us plenty of time for some more fun."

Normally I wouldn't. I'd already fucked this little plaything six ways from Sunday when we'd come home from the club last night. She'd had the best night of her life to date; anything else was just greedy on her part.

But then I remembered. *The news will be out in two weeks.*

I didn't have long left to live a normal lifestyle. Might as well make the most of it.

"What's your name?" I asked. I didn't want to give commands to "the blonde" all morning.

A glimmer of disappointment flashed across her face as she realized I'd forgotten her name, but she moved past it quick enough.

"Sabrina," she replied.

"Okay, Sabrina. How about you go introduce yourself to my cock?"

Sabrina smiled as she whipped off the cover and crawled down between my legs. Her tiny hand wrapped around my shaft, before she leant down and licked my tip with her warm tongue.

"You like that, baby?" Sabrina asked sweetly, as she stroked my cock.

"Yeah, real good, darling," I replied. "Now suck it." I slipped my fingers into her hair and pushed her down to my member in case she needed any further encouragement.

Sabrina's mouth opened just in time to receive my cock. Her tongue pressed against my length as she sucked so hard she almost drew the cum out of me immediately. My tip hit the back of her throat, and she barely batted an eyelash.

This girl knew what she was doing. She'd earned the right to take control for a few minutes. I lay back and closed my eyes while Sabrina's head bobbed up and down on my cock. She moaned and gasped each time she came up for air, but showed no sign of stopping. A trail of saliva hung from her lips and ended at my cock. That was enough for me.

Her wet mouth was just the starter. Now I wanted the main course.

I grabbed her hair again and pulled her off my cock, pushing her to one side so that she fell flat on her back with her legs open ready for me. Sabrina leaned over and grabbed a condom from the bedside table and slipped it from its foil wrapper. Women putting the condom on could be sexy as hell, but more often than not, it wasn't worth the hassle. I grabbed the condom from her and quickly rolled it down my member before plunging my cock deep into her eager wet slit.

Sabrina groaned eagerly, as her eyes closed and her head snapped back, like I'd sent an electric shock up her spine.

It was nearly impossible to have a headache when a tight, wet pussy was wrapped around your cock. Her breasts heaved with every thrust, and her groans turned to screams as I delved deeper and deeper inside her.

I grabbed hold of her wrists and held them above her head, looking in her eyes as I pounded her with hard, deep thrusts. I brought her to the edge within minutes, and unlike last night, I didn't have the patience to stretch it out. With my cock nestled inside her sex, I rocked my hips firmly against hers, rubbing her clit as my cock throbbed inside her. Her orgasm came quickly and loudly. She screamed in my ear, threatening to bring back my headache, as she spasmed under my firm grip.

While Sabrina shook on the bed, I lifted up her legs, pressing her knees up by her ears, as I watched my cock sliding in and out of her wet, bare sex. She looked so pure and virginal; I knew better.

I growled deeply as I came, keeping my cock deep inside her tight pussy as jet after jet of my spunk poured forth.

I collapsed down onto Sabrina, before remembering that I had no intention of lingering here any longer than I had to. I pulled out, carefully making sure the condom stayed on, and then went to the bathroom to dispose of it along with all the others. She had quite the collection of used condoms in there now.

They might be valuable in a few weeks, I thought, as I remembered the ticking time bomb that was due to go off soon and change my life forever.

A loud knocking on her door reminded me that I needed to get the hell out of here and quick. "Sabrina, are you ready?"

"Just coming," she yelled.

"Again?" I asked. "I'm not even touching you this time."

She threw my pants and trousers at me playfully, and I remembered that I shouldn't be joking around with women like her.

"Do you live local?" Sabrina asked.

And that's why.

"Relatively," I replied, letting it hang in the air.

"Do you go to Tonic often?"

I used to, but I won't be able to anymore. Not after the news is out in the open.

"Not really."

I dressed quickly before things got even more awkward. I threw on my jeans and a shirt, not even bothering to stick my boxers on first. They just got shoved in a pocket, along with my socks. My shoes were on and I had my hand on the doorknob when she caught up with me.

"Why don't you come by tomorrow night?" Sabrina asked. "We're having a party on this floor, so it's not like we'll even have to go far if we want to... sneak away."

"I can't make tomorrow night."

I opened the door and started to shuffle out. I really didn't want her to be too pissed off with me if I could avoid it, but I was a shitty liar as well.

"Am I going to see you again?"

This time her voice was weak with emotion. Some girls got mad, some got upset. This one was a crier.

The news will be out in two weeks. Maybe sooner.

"You are definitely going to see me again," I said honestly.

"I am?" she asked with a big grin on her face. She looked almost as happy now as she had done when I'd had my dick inside her.

"Yes. And real soon, I promise. You'll be sick of the sight of me by the end of the month."

I couldn't lie, but I could sure as shit bend the truth.

I stormed straight past Sabrina's friend in the hall—hopefully quickly enough that she wouldn't recognize me later—and headed down the stairs. I'd been in this building plenty of times before and knew my way out.

More importantly, I knew my way to the café on campus. It would be full of students, but it was also full of coffee and right now my need for caffeine surpassed my desire not to listen to students talk bollocks. Just.

Only two weeks left now.

Two more weeks of freedom, and then my life would change forever.

Chapter Two

SOPHIA

"Soy milk latte for Thomas," I called out over the sound of fingers moving furiously across keyboards.

Ten minutes until my break.

I eyed the few remaining free tables, hoping that my evil stare would stop other students from sitting at them. It didn't work.

What good was a break if I couldn't use it to get some work done? We were a whopping two months into the semester—or 'term,' as they called it here—and I was already behind on my studies.

The scariest part was that I only had six more months to go before finishing my master's degree. A year abroad had sounded like a long time when I'd been back in California. The plan had been to come here and get a degree, and then stay to work for an English company. Unfortunately, that meant getting a visa, and they weren't exactly giving them out like candy any more. Time was running out fast. If I didn't get a visa soon, then I'd be heading back home to a lifetime of bad memories and a mother who was still pissed at me.

I'd come to England to get over Stan by hooking up with cute English guys, and I'd done just that. Okay, not all of them had been that cute, but it was better than sitting alone in my room and wallowing in self-pity.

Now I didn't want to go home.

"You're daydreaming again, babe," Ellie whispered in my ear.

I came to my senses and saw a man—presumably Thomas—waiting for me to hand over his soy latte.

"Sorry," I muttered, as I handed over the drink.

"Still dreaming about your Prince Charming?" Ellie teased.

She knew I'd come to England hoping to be swept off my feet by a Benedict Cumberbatch look-alike. The closest I'd come was taking a drink order from someone who looked a bit like a younger, uglier Martin Freeman.

"There's still time," I replied. "You must have some charming men around here."

"If there are, I ain't found any of them. And let me tell you, that one you locked lips with last night was no Prince Charming."

"Yeah," I agreed. "Turns out not all the frogs turn into princes after a kiss."

"I might be able to hook you up with a friend tomorrow night if you're interested?"

"No, thank you," I replied immediately. "I'm still having nightmares about the last guy you set me up with. You told me he looked like a famous soccer player."

"*Football* player," she corrected. "And I wasn't lying."

"Yes, but you failed to tell me that the *soccer* player in question was Wayne Rooney."

"You wouldn't have known who he was, even if I had told you."

"I could have googled him. I turned up expecting to meet someone who looked like David Beckham."

Ellie laughed loudly, and then quickly covered her mouth as the customers looked up to glare at her. "Okay, fair play, that guy was a bit of a stinker. Tell you the truth, he was sniffing around me so I used you to get him off my case."

"Have I told you what a good friend you are lately?"

"No, you haven't said that in a while."

"Yeah, go figure."

The rush of customers had died down now that lectures for the day had started, but a few more wandered in looking worse for wear. It was the same every Friday morning. Thursday night was the big student night at the local club, and we were still far enough from exams that people were going to every event they could hoping to hook up.

I'd been one of them. I'd even latched on to a nice enough guy who seemed capable of holding a conversation. But he kept drinking. And drinking. Eventually he ended up not even knowing the way home. If he didn't know the way home, he wouldn't know the way to anything else important. No thank you.

The café I worked in was staffed nearly entirely by students, and most of them were clever enough to insist on not working Fridays. I hadn't known any better when I started, so now I always had to work one of the busiest and most understaffed shifts available. Wasn't I lucky?

"Let's go out tonight," Ellie said, while we stood next to each other pouring coffees. The smell of fresh coffee did wonders for my hangover, but the heat made me sweaty and sticky. Not a particularly attractive combination.

"I went out last night," I replied.

"I know, I was there. You're a student. You're supposed to go out all the time."

"Yes, but I'm a mature student. I don't have the energy for that any more."

"You're twenty-three, Sophia. Not fifty-three."

I considered it for a moment, but shook my head. Every night was the same. It would start well. Guys would smile at me, some of them would come over. We'd chat, we'd flirt, we'd kiss.

And then someone would suggest doing shots.

British men could certainly handle their drink, but they didn't know their limits. The men would egg each other on until they were all "completely plastered," and that would be the end of my dreams for the evening.

I wouldn't quite say I regretted coming to England, but it hadn't been all I'd hoped for either. It was still better than what I'd left behind; a broken engagement, and a broken heart.

"You're coming," Ellie insisted.

"Why? So I can meet more immature students?" I grabbed the finished coffee and walked back to the counter. "Americano for Laura," I yelled out, as I slapped the coffee down and took another order.

"We're not going to a student club," Ellie continued when I made it back to the cappuccino machine. "Dani got us into Viva. It's over twenty-ones only, so the clientèle is a little more upmarket."

"Can't be that upmarket if they're letting you in."

"I will have you know," Ellie said, putting on a posh, upper-class accent, "I can be perfectly sublime when I go to the effort." She flicked her hair for good measure, before reverting back to her normal voice. "Plus, Dani sucked off the bouncer last night, so he'll let us in."

"I don't know... I have so much work to do."

"I'm not taking no for an answer. This place is uber-sophisticated. They don't sell any drinks that cost less than £10."

"Well now you've sold me," I replied sarcastically. "I can spend an entire month's wages in one night."

Ellie rolled her eyes, but another customer appeared before she could reply. Ellie disappeared to take the order, while I tried—and failed—to make a flower in the foam of the coffee. How did people do that?

"Why do people order tea in a place like this?" Ellie asked after serving the customer. "We're literally just sticking a tea bag in hot water. How lazy do you have to be not to do that at home? I mean, it's one thing if you're making a proper brew with milk and all, but this is just green tea."

She poured some hot water, and walked back to the counter with a big smile. "Here you go," she said cheerfully to the customer she'd just insulted. For a brief moment, I thought I'd escaped a lecture, but I should have known better. "Look, you're always complaining about not meeting charming English gentleman. That's because you've been looking in the wrong places. I mean, look around here." Ellie waved an arm around the café. "Hardly a prize pool, is it?"

"I guess not," I admitted.

Most of the guys here were friendly enough, but I had to admit that none of them excited me in any way. I recognized a few from class, but a lot of them were undergrads. They were only a couple of years younger than me, but it made a huge difference.

"We need to meet some older gentleman," Ellie said. "Ones who know how to treat a lady."

"And you," I joked.

"I can be a lady, thank you very much. Right up until the moment I get them naked that is."

A smile crept across my face, but I quickly shook it off. "I can't afford it."

"Sophia, I don't know how things work in your country, but over here pretty young things like us don't have to pay for our own drinks. We'll just sit there at the bar and wait for men to come over."

Ellie turned her back to me and went to serve a customer before I could argue. Typical. She appeared by my side again before I'd even had time to sigh in frustration.

"I'll do you a deal," she said excitedly. "I'll let you serve the next customer, if you agree to come out tonight."

I must have misheard her. "Wait, you want me to do *more* work, and in return you get what you want?"

"Trust me on this," she added with a wink. "You're going to want to serve the next customer."

I didn't have the energy to argue, and at least work kept me busy. I walked toward the customer, brushing the chocolate dust from my hands onto my apron as I did so.

Then I looked up at the man waiting in line.
Oh. Shit.

Chapter Three

GEORGE

"What can I get you?" the young brunette asked. Was that an American accent?

Boy, did I wake up in the wrong bed this morning. Sabrina was cute, but this barista was stunning. An apron stopped me getting a decent view of her cleavage, but she had her sleeves rolled up revealing soft, tanned skin. More tanned than I usually saw in the north of England.

Loose strands of hair clung to her face where she'd been sweating, no doubt caused by the steam pouring out of the coffee machines. It was a look I wouldn't mind seeing again in my bed.

"I'll have an Americano," I said, just as she started to look a little creeped out by me staring at her. "But put two shots of espresso in there. And then I'll have an espresso on the side as well." I looked at her name badge and added "thank you, Sophia."

"What's your name?" Sophia asked.

"George. You want my phone number too?"

She rolled her eyes and held up the coffee cup, making sure I could see her write my name on it in marker pen.

"Where's that accent from?" I asked.

"I'm American," she said softly.

"Oh, I'm sorry. Well, it can't be helped. Where exactly are you from? I'm guessing California."

"Good guess," she replied. "Most people assume I'm from New York for some reason."

"Most people are idiots," I said as I tapped my card against the machine to pay. "You don't sound anything like a New Yorker."

I couldn't claim to be a huge fan of the New York accent, but I was a fan of the women. I'd had some mind-blowing experiences with New Yorkers, but—other than a certain actress—I couldn't recall shagging any Californians. That might have to change, and what better place to start than the one right here on my doorstep?

"Are you a student here?" I asked. If she was, she must be close to graduating, because she was at least twenty-one, if not older. The eighteen-year-old from last night—and this morning—had been fun, but I did crave a little more experience in a woman.

"Yes," Sophia said, as she handed me a receipt. "I'll go make your drinks."

"I'll do them," a cheerful voice called out from behind Sophia. "Americano with a double shot, and then a shot of espresso on the side."

"Thanks, Ellie," Sophia said curtly, in a way that made it clear Ellie's help was not in fact appreciated.

"Do you want them for here or to go?" Ellie called out to me.

"You know, I was going to get them to go, but all of a sudden I have a desire to stay."

My hangover wouldn't be helped by the irritating sound of students typing furiously on laptops while listening to shitty music on headphones. However, I only had two more weeks. I had to take any opportunity to have fun while I still could.

"How long will you be in England for?" I asked.

"Another six months. I'm studying for my masters."

Six months? Interesting. Six months was about how long I needed to be married for to claim my inheritance. That's what Alisa and I had agreed to do until she went and bailed on me.

I was getting ahead of myself. So far she didn't even look interested in serving me my coffee, let alone anything else.

"Sampled any of the local delicacies yet?" I asked with a suggestive smile.

"Are you talking about food, or... something else?"

"Let's say I'm talking about food."

"Okay. I've tried some of the local *food*."

Why did I feel a weird sensation in my chest when she said that? That was a new one. I'd never been bothered by women talking about other men before.

"What did you think?" I asked the question, although I wasn't sure I wanted to hear the answer.

"Let's just say the appetizers were non-existent, the main course was over rather quickly, and I never even saw a dessert menu."

"Portion sizes?"

"So far I really do believe everything is bigger in America."

"I'm disappointed in my fellow countrymen," I said honestly. I didn't like to think of her with other men, but at the very least they should have kept her satisfied. This was a woman who deserved orgasm after orgasm until she was too exhausted to move. I was already picturing just how I would arrange that.

I stepped closer to the counter to hide the bulge in my trousers that threatened to make itself known ahead of schedule.

"How about I take you out to a restaurant where the appetizers are just as good—if not better—than the main course, and you are guaranteed to finish your meal before I do."

"Tempting," she replied. "But I think I'll pass. You look like a guy who has eaten at all the food joints on campus and probably most of the restaurants in the city too."

Ellie came over with the coffee, but she looked reluctant to interrupt our conversation. That told me everything I needed to know. Sophia was going through a dry spell, and her friend wanted to help her out.

It also told me that Sophia was stubborn, because she was doing her best to fend me off. That wouldn't last long, but I admired her for trying.

I grabbed my coffee, and took a seat at the only empty table in the place. I moved the seat so that I could sit with my back to the wall and look up at Sophia between sips of my coffee.

She'd seen what was on the menu, and wouldn't be able to resist for long. She was hungry, and a Michelin star restaurant was offering her a three course meal. It was only a matter of time before she caved.

_-*-_

Hurry up, Sophia. I can only make this coffee last so long.

I'd necked the espresso back like I was an idiot student downing shots to impress women at the bar. That had sparked part of my brain back to life, but not enough that I could actually concentrate on emails or work.

Not that I really had a job at the moment. Not unless you counted 'trying to convince the trustee of Mum's estate to hand over my inheritance,' as a full-time job. I needed to get my hands on that money soon, or I'd have to give in to my destiny and ruin my life. Either way, I needed money desperately to pay off debts, and I couldn't hang around forever.

The news will be out in two weeks.

My plan with Alisa had been nearly foolproof. 'Nearly' being the crucial word. Alisa would marry me, hang around for six months, and then disappear. By that time, I'd have claimed my inheritance, and she'd have a nice, tidy sum for her troubles.

Everybody won.

But then Alisa backed out, and soon I'd be more screwed than a waitress serving coffee to Tiger Woods.

I should have had a back-up plan in place, but now it was too late.

The doors opened as groups of students started milling in while having a heated discussion about some BS social issue of the week. The first class of the day must have just finished, which meant I'd been here about an hour already. Most of that time had been spent looking at Sophia.

Time well spent, I'd say.

I'd caught her staring at me a few times as well. One minute, she appeared shy and reserved, and the next she looked hard-edged and determined. Maybe she was all those things. All I knew for sure was that she was beautiful. Anyone who could look that good while preparing coffee in unflattering clothes and an apron definitely deserved my attention, and a hell of a lot more besides.

Three girls burst into the café in a triangle formation, like you saw on American teen movies. Leader at the front—typical head cheerleader type—with two hangers on just behind her. They walked past the counter and appeared to be heading straight for me. It wasn't unusual for women to make a beeline for me, but they looked mad. Friends of Sabrina perhaps?

"I know what you did last night," one of the women yelled loudly.

I opened my mouth to tell her it was none of her business, but then realized she wasn't talking to me. Her words were aimed at a girl sat down at the table next to me. She'd been working studiously on something that was

21

either a maths problem, or a translation of an alien language. Same thing in my book.

The girl pulled headphones out of her ears, and looked up nervously. "What's going on?"

"Don't play fucking innocent with me, Jody. You shagged Abib last night."

"I—"

"And don't deny it. He's already told the entire chemistry class what a slut you are."

I caught Sophia looking on anxiously, as were most of the students. Sophia probably felt right at home, because this was like a scene straight from an American high school. At least, it was if *Mean Girls* was in any way accurate, and I assumed it was. Hollywood movies never lied.

"It's none of your business what I did," the girl responded. She tried her best to sound defiant, but it wasn't convincing anyone. I could tell immediately that she had slept with this Abib guy, and she looked embarrassed by the entire situation.

She didn't need to be. She was a student. She'd had sex. How was that something to be ashamed about in this day and age?

"It is *my* fucking business," the leader yelled back. I assumed her name was Regina. "You knew I liked him."

Oh bloody hell, this was pathetic.

"Excuse me, love," I said calmly, but not quietly. "Some of us are trying to work here. Can't you have this conversation over Snapchat or something?"

"No," the girl snapped back, standing up straight. "Because I want the whole uni to know that Jody is a slut."

"I'm not—"

"You're a whore."

Jody looked a little closer to tears now. Far too close for my liking. Her strong façade had been quickly stripped away by the twenty or so pairs of eyes now focused on her.

"Let me get this straight," I said calmly. "You think Jody is a slut, because she slept with a guy you wanted to sleep with."

"That's literally the dictionary definition of the word slut."

Hm, incorrect use of the word 'literally.' Had I been teleported to America overnight?

"But you would have slept with him if you could?" I asked.

"Well, yes, but—"

"So if Jody is a slut for sleeping with him, what does that make you? A slut-in-training? An apprentice slut? I'm a Star Wars fan, so I like the term 'Padawan.' Perhaps you could be Jody's Padawan and she'll teach you how to trick guys into actually sleeping with you."

"This is none of your business," one of the girl's friends—let's call her Gretchen—yelled out from behind her.

"It is my business, because some of us have work to do, and we could do without idiots coming in and shouting their mouths off." *Speechless. Lovely.* "Run along, children."

The girls turned on their heels in almost perfect unison, and stormed off. I cast a stern gaze around the café to make sure that anyone who'd been watching the show quickly went back to their work, or typing on their phones. No doubt this would be all over Facebook within thirty seconds if it wasn't already.

"Thank you," Jody said softly. "You didn't need to step in for me."

"I'm sure you could have handled it, but I have a passionate hatred for slut-shaming."

"I didn't take you for the feminist type."

"Oh, I'm not. I just have a vested interest in women not being slut-shamed." Jody frowned in confusion. "I want women to feel comfortable having one-night-stands. It works out to my benefit, if you get my drift."

"Ah," she said with a smile. "Yeah, I get you." Just as I was about to go back to my work, she added "I didn't screw him."

"I honestly don't care either way."

"I tried to, but he couldn't get it up."

"And now he's trying to make you look bad because he's scared you'll tell people?"

"I guess."

"I'm sure he was kind and considerate enough to take care of your needs though?"

"Oh sure," she said. "He gave me a brolly so I didn't have to walk back to my room in the rain."

I laughed. "By the standards of this place, he's practically a gentleman."

"Unfortunately you're right. Anyway, I'll let you get back to work."

Jody put her headphones back on and I went back to watching Sophia. Except Sophia wasn't there anymore.

I looked around, but she was nowhere to be seen. Surely she hadn't snuck off without so much as a goodbye?

Then I saw her.

She came out of the back room carrying a notepad and a couple of textbooks. I watched as she cast her gaze around the room looking for somewhere to sit.

There was only one chair left in the entire place. And it just so happened to be right opposite me.

Chapter Four

SOPHIA

We needed a staff-only table in this place. The staff room out back was far too hot and stuffy to study in, so I had to come out here with everyone else. Except there was only one seat free, and three guesses who was sitting at that table.

Ellie had let me serve George thinking she was doing me a favor. If the job involved just looking at him then I would have been grateful. Unfortunately, when he spoke, his words drove me crazy. And not in a good way.

He had the posh English accent most Americans assumed everyone here spoke with, but while he sounded charming as hell, his words made him sound like an arrogant douchebag. If I'd wanted one of them I would have stayed in America.

Even by student standards, he looked roughly kept and disheveled, but damn he could pull it off. He had serious bed head, and the bags under his eyes suggested he hadn't gotten much sleep, but somehow that look suited him.

The lack of sleep could no doubt be traced back to a female student who lived on campus. The slim-fit shirt he wore—with more buttons undone than done up—had so many creases, it was obvious he'd thrown it to the floor in a hurry the night before.

The lack of a jacket even though it was about to rain also screamed "walk of shame." He probably wouldn't like that term though. Not judging by the way he'd stood up for Jody. The coffee shop was supposedly full of liberal, modern students, but George had been the only one to do anything about that little scene. Everyone else had just stood back and watched—me included.

George waved me over, motioning to the empty seat opposite him. I triple checked the rest of the tables to see if anyone else might be leaving, but everyone was settled in for the day.

I had no choice.

I walked over to George's table and set my books down loudly. I wanted him to know I was only here for one thing, and it wasn't to continue our conversation.

"Hi," he said, a big grin etched across his face. He sat back in his chair, with one ankle resting on the other knee as he sipped at a coffee that must surely be empty by now.

"Hi," I replied, looking down at my books and frantically opening the page to where I'd left off. I had a hundred pages of reading to do before I could even make a start on the three-thousand-word essay that was due in two weeks. I didn't have time for anything—or anyone—else right now.

"Glad you could join me."

"I'm not joining you. I'm sitting here to work."

"So I see. What's the topic?"

"The English Civil War."

"Ah, a favorite topic of mine."

"You like English history?" I asked incredulously. He didn't exactly look like the history type. He was more the type to fake an interest to get in someone's panties. Was that what he was doing now?

26

I crossed my legs under the table. No time for thoughts like that.

"I like most history up until the end of the English civil wars actually. After that it starts becoming too focused on politics. I can read about kings and queens all day, but prime ministers send me to sleep."

"Wars?" I asked. "You said English civil *wars*. Plural. There was only one."

George gave a shrug of the shoulders. "I'd say there were three, but it depends how you define it. People lump the separate conflicts together and refer to it as a war, but that's not really accurate. So what's your essay on?"

Was this really the same guy who had spoken to me earlier? They seemed like two different people. I didn't have any special interest in English history—I'd only chosen it because it seemed like the logical thing to study in England—but I could listen to George talk all day. If I had professors like him, it wouldn't be so difficult to stay awake in class. Without the arrogant words, his smooth voice was like a drug that made me sleepy and aroused at the same time. Either way, I'd be heading to bed.

"Nothing," I replied, snapping out of my trance. "I mean, we can choose what to write about."

"And what are you going to write about?"

"I don't know yet. I still have loads of reading to do."

"If I didn't know better, I'd swear you were already getting in your excuses for turning me down later."

"I don't need an excuse to do that," I replied. "Besides, I'm already going out with friends tonight."

"I want to see you again."

The word 'okay' was on the tip of my tongue, and came desperately close to escaping my lips. Would it really be such a bad idea to see him again? He was as easy on the eyes as he was on the ears. He was older than the other students, and didn't look like the type to down shots at the end of the night.

He was the 'Prince Charming' I'd been looking for, but maybe that's not what I wanted after all. I'd told everyone back home that I was going to England to meet a nice English guy and settle down, but that was only half the story. I was also escaping my past heartbreak.

I'd been concentrating so much on finding a man, that I hadn't dealt with the shame I still felt for what happened with Stan. Maybe I wasn't ready to move on just yet.

"No," I replied eventually. I couldn't be taken in by a nice accent and a handsome face. And nice arms. Strong shoulders. Deep, dark eyes. "I have too much work to do."

He looked surprised, as if he hadn't heard the word 'no' in a very long time. "The hard bit is finding a title for the essay," he said, quickly moving on past my rejection. "Once you've got that, the rest will flow easily."

"Sure. But like you said, finding the title is the hard part."

"I'll make you a deal," he said. "If I give you an essay title and some pointers on what to discuss, you agree to go out with me tomorrow night."

"I can't go out three nights in a row," I pleaded. My brain was already begging me to get an early night. However, face-to-face with George, other parts of my body were making pleas of their own.

"I'll have you in bed by ten. Whether you choose to sleep or not is up to you. Do we have a deal?"

I looked up to the ceiling and then back down with an overly-dramatic sigh. "Okay, but it had better be a good title."

"It'll more than suffice. Call it 'The Fallacy of the English Civil War.' You can split it into two sections: first, the fact that the war wasn't English. It involved

Scotland, Ireland, and Wales too. People often look past that. Second, it wasn't just one war. If you want, you can talk about how history has chosen to refer to it in a way that promotes English dominance over other nations, blah, blah, blah."

"That sounds… better than anything I could have come up with."

"Good, then it's a date. I'll meet you outside here at eight."

"It's not a date," I said firmly. "I'm just going to have a drink with you to thank you for your help, and also to thank you for shutting up so that I can get on with my reading."

"Fine with me," he replied. "I just want to enjoy my last couple of weeks of freedom."

"Huh?"

"Nothing. I'll leave you to it."

I stared at the page in front of me, refusing to turn and watch him walk away. The words wouldn't sink in. I wasn't entirely sure what had just happened, but I should be able to get out of it easy enough. I could fake being ill on Saturday if necessary.

I sure as hell couldn't go on a date with George. I could handle the drunken idiots, but I wasn't sure I'd be able to handle him, and that had me scared.

Maybe I didn't want to meet Prince Charming after all. I was just running from my past. The last thing I wanted to do was repeat my mistakes.

Wasn't that exactly why we studied history in the first place? To learn from our mistakes.

Those ignorant of history are doomed to repeat it. I knew my history, and I was determined not to repeat it.

Chapter Five

GEORGE

It wasn't often I smiled when walking across a university campus, but no amount of students could make me miserable now.

A text from my favorite journalist sure could though.

The leak will happen soon. Real soon. Sorry, there was nothing I could do. Editor's orders.

Shit.

Shit, shit, shit.

How soon? I asked in reply.

Maybe tomorrow.

Fucking bloody shit. I couldn't go out with Sophia tomorrow night. Even if the news hadn't leaked by the evening, she'd wake up to find a hundred photographers outside her door or mine, depending on where we ended up. No country had a press quite like that of Britain. They were ruthless, and they'd be on me, and anyone I was with, in an instant.

I had to see Sophia again. I didn't just want to squeeze in a little more fun before the news leaked. I wanted to squeeze in a little more fun *with her* before the news leaked. I doubled back and snuck into the café without her noticing. She was still on her break, studying hard, although she hadn't turned the page yet. Slow reader perhaps.

Sophia had been talking to another barista when I'd come in and they seemed to be close. Can't hurt to try.

I walked up to the counter and under my breath introduced myself to a woman called Ellie.

"Did you get anywhere with Sophia?" Ellie asked quietly.

"Yes, but there's been a change of plans. Do you know where she's going to be tonight?"

"Oh yeah, I think I can help with that."

_-*-_

"I wish you would stop stressing about all this and see the positive side," Tabitha said. My half-sister lived in America now, but that hadn't stopped her being addicted to tea and biscuits. Even over the video chat, I could see her dunking something resembling a bourbon into her tea.

"There is no positive side," I insisted. "Our lives are about to get turned upside down. Worst of all, I'm going to end up bringing you and Liam into this mess."

"It's not your fault. You can't help who your father is. Besides, as I keep telling you, you don't owe us anything. Stop stressing."

How could she appear so calm all the time? Tabitha could barely get around the house by herself, let alone look after her young son. Yet every time we spoke she always sounded like the happy one, while I was miserable and determined to find a way to fix all my sister's problems.

"I won't stop stressing until I've fixed this mess," I replied. "I'm going to get my inheritance, and then I'll sort everything."

"You need to let go," Tabitha said calmly. "Your engagement to Alisa collapsed—thank God—so now you're not going to get your hands on that inheritance.

Time's almost up. Not unless you ensnare some poor girl in your scheme in the next few..."

She trailed off when she saw the look on my face on her laptop.

"There's still time, sis. You know me, never say never."

Tabitha was right, but I couldn't accept that yet. There had to be a way out of this. The problem wasn't even that complicated when you boiled it down to the basics. Liam and Tabitha had medical bills—big ones. They needed money. I had to get money. Tabitha and I had different fathers, but mine had put a nice little sum away in a trust. After Mum's death, that money became mine, or at least it would if I could satisfy one simple condition—get married by the time I'm twenty-five. Simple.

And if I couldn't get the money that way, there was always plan B.

I hated the idea of marriage—I was a walking male cliché in that respect—but I hated plan B even more. Marriage was my idea of heaven in comparison. A wife might be a ball and chain, but plan B would be a ball and chain, plus I'd be locked up in a dungeon, with the key thrown into the ocean. Or maybe I'd just be locked up in the Tower of London. I didn't even like London.

"You don't need to do all this for us," Tabitha said. "Liam is my responsibility not yours. And it's not your fault I didn't get left much in the will. My biological father wasn't quite as rich as yours."

"Few people are," I said softly. "Look, we've had this conversation before, and I'm not going to change my mind now. I'll do whatever it takes to make sure you and Liam are set for life."

"Even if you have to get married to do it?"

"You haven't seen the woman I have in mind. It wouldn't be much of a sacrifice."

_*_

33

By the time I arrived at Viva, Sophia, Ellie, and another girl, were already chatting to three guys who were buying them drinks.

The three girls were tarted up to the nines, but it was only Sophia who had my attention. She wore a short black skirt that glittered slightly when caught by the lights, and clung tightly to her body. Her legs had a light golden tan that many of the women around here tried—and failed—to match with less natural tanning methods.

She wore a white halterneck top with a plunging neckline, but I couldn't make out much of her chest. That would have to be a treat for later.

Much as I had done earlier today in the coffee shop, I sat at a table and enjoyed the view. The only difference was that this time I sipped whiskey and not coffee.

I felt an unusual pang of what I assumed was jealousy in my chest as I watched Sophia chatting to the guy closest to her. The three guys looked like they were investment bankers, but there weren't many of them in York. That meant they were dressing in pinstripe suits and loud ties because they *wanted* to look like investment bankers. That said all you needed to know about these three.

Sophia kept smiling at the guy talking to her, but there were no other signs of attraction. I was an expert at reading women's body language, and there was no way she wanted this guy.

She took regular sips of her drink as he spoke, suggesting she was bored stiff by the conversation. She nodded along at regular intervals, but only to look like she was still paying attention. Finally, her chest pointed more towards the bar than the guy. If she wanted to capture his attention, one flash of those things would have him drooling and buying her all the drinks she wanted. The fact that she didn't bother spoke volumes.

I couldn't relax. I polished off one glass of whiskey, and ordered another from a waitress hanging around close by. It was no good. I couldn't enjoy the whiskey while Sophia was chatting to this moron in a suit.

I made my move and headed to the bar. As luck would have it, the three men decided it was a good time to go to the toilets. And I thought only women went together. Probably planning on doing a few lines while they're in there. Classy places like this were just the same as grungy bars. The guys snorted more expensive drugs and wore better clothes, but it was all the same at the end of the day.

Ellie caught sight of me approaching and smiled excitedly. She clearly hadn't told Sophia I would be here tonight.

"Good evening, Sophia," I said, approaching her from behind. I placed a hand on the soft skin of her back and bent forward slightly to kiss her on the cheek. "It's so nice to see you again."

"What the hell." She spun around in her seat and kicked me in the shins in the process. "Oops, sorry."

"No problem," I lied, as the pain gradually faded.

"What are you doing here? We said tomorrow night."

"Yeah, but I'm an impatient guy."

"Anyone going to introduce me?" the third girl asked.

"Dani, this is George," Ellie said.

"How do you know his name?" Sophia asked her friend. "Nevermind. His presence here tonight has your name written all over it."

"You're welcome," Ellie said dryly. "Would you rather keep talking to Whit?"

"God no," Sophia replied quickly.

"Those men not to your tastes?" I asked the girls.

"No," Ellie said just as quickly as Sophia had.

35

"I'm going through a dry spell," Dani said. "But even so, I'm not going near them tonight. I might let them buy me one more drink and that's it."

I leaned forward and whispered in Sophia's ear, making sure to get a glimpse of her delicious cleavage in the process. "Want me to get rid of him?"

Sophia sighed, but then nodded. "But that doesn't mean I want you either, just to be clear."

"Message understood. Loud and clear."

I glanced over at the toilets and saw the three of them coming back.

"Just remember," I said to Sophia, "you asked for this."

"Asked for—"

The rest of her words were muffled by my lips as I leant in and kissed her.

Chapter Six

SOPHIA

"Whoa." Ellie sounded as shocked as I felt.

I leaned back in my seat as George's lips pressed up against mine, and his hand caressed my face. I forgot what to do. I'd kissed a guy just last night, yet this felt more like my first kiss ever.

Excitement. Nerves. Fear. More excitement. Lust. They all crashed and collided together, as George's lips parted mine just wide enough so that his tongue could reach inside and touch my own.

Some of my senses came back to me. My hands dangled limply by my side, so I wrapped them around his large torso and placed them on his muscular back.

Faint hints of his aftershave wafted up my nose, as I tried to focus on what they hell I was doing. Eyes closed. Check. Lips moving. Check. Heart racing. Double check.

I knew I was in a bar, with my friends watching on excitedly, but in my mind, we were in the privacy of my bedroom. The music that had been pumping so loud we could barely hear each other, lowered to a slow, soothing rhythm. The chair I was perched on became the edge of the bed on which I'd soon be experiencing ecstasy as George took me—

He stopped kissing me as abruptly as he'd started. "They've gone now," he said.

I opened my eyes and tried to regain my focus. I felt like I'd been in the dark for days, and my eyes were trying to adjust to sunlight, instead of the rather dim lights in the club.

George was having no such issues. He took a sip of his drink, and acted like nothing had happened. He had on another shirt, although this time most of the buttons were done up, and it had been ironed. His jeans still looked a little rough, but perhaps that was the fashion now. At least he didn't look like those douchebags who'd been hanging around us before he scared them off. They didn't stop talking about how rich they were, which either meant they were tools or liars. Likely both, actually.

George had done us a favor, but that didn't make this any less weird. At least I could count on Ellie and Dani to acknowledge how bat shit crazy this all was.

Holy shit, Ellie mouthed, when I looked over at her.

I couldn't quite tell what Dani was trying to say, but it looked a lot like "fuck him." She did tend to get to the point.

"Thanks George," Ellie said. "For getting rid of those assholes. Although they were about to buy us another drink, so I reckon you owe us one."

"Ellie," I snapped. "We can buy our own damn drinks."

That's what overdrafts were for.

George laughed, and waved for the attention of a nearby barmaid, who seemed ready and willing to serve him at a second's notice.

"These three ladies are drinking on me tonight," he said casually.

"Yes, Mr. Whittemore."

"You really don't have to do that," I insisted.

"Don't worry about it," George replied. "At least this way you only have to spend the evening talking to one arrogant arse."

"I suggest we all drink some expensive whiskey," Ellie said. "I've always wondered what whiskey tastes like when it's not mixed with coke or lemonade."

"Four of these," George said to the barmaid, as he held up his drink. "The drinks come with one condition," he added.

I sighed, and slumped back down in my seat. "Men always expect something in return. Usually one thing in particular."

"I don't care," Dani said quickly. "I'll do whatever you want me to. All three of us will, won't we girls? I'm sure we won't mind getting to know each other a little more intimately."

Ellie laughed, while I choked back what was left of my cocktail.

"I appreciate the enthusiasm, but actually all I wanted was a little one-on-one time with Sophia. Nothing seedy. I just want to get to know her a little better. Deal?"

"Sounds great," Ellie said.

"I suppose," Dani said disappointedly.

"Do I get any say in this?" I asked. Ellie and Dani both stared at me like I was mad. I realized they were probably right. Why was I fighting this? I was being contrarian for the sake of it. If Ellie and Dani had told me George was a jerk, I'd be all over him like a rash.

"Uh, you ladies discuss it," George said. He was looking towards the far end of the bar where the three men were now standing. It looked like they were talking to some new victims, but I couldn't see because of a pillar in the way. "I'll be right back."

George walked towards the group while the barmaid poured us each a double measure of whiskey from the top shelf. It looked like liquid money. Like $100 bills—or £50 notes I suppose—melted down and poured into a glass.

It smelled like success.

It tasted like… like fire.

"Holy shit," I coughed, after taking a sip. "This stuff is strong."

"People drink this for pleasure?" Ellie asked after taking a sip herself.

"I like it," Dani said, despite cringing when she took a sip. "It tastes like money. Speaking of which…"

"Yeah, what the hell is the deal with this George guy?" Ellie asked.

"I should be asking you," I replied. "I assume his appearance here is not a coincidence?"

"Well, no, but I didn't know you guys were that close already."

"We're not," I insisted. "That was just… I don't know what that was."

"That was the prelude to a lot of hot sex," Dani insisted.

"It was just a kiss," I said.

The best kiss I'd had since coming to England. I cast my mind back to other first kisses I'd had in America, but there hadn't been any like that. Not even close.

"That wasn't just a kiss," Ellie said. "I've seen you kiss guys before, and it doesn't look like that."

"I didn't know you paid such close attention to my technique."

Ellie shrugged and took another sip of her whiskey, even though she still clearly hated the taste. "There wasn't much technique that time. You looked like a fish out of water."

"He took me by surprise," I said defensively.

"Well now you've had time to prepare, so you can up your game. Stop being so cold around him."

"She's right," Dani said. "You're always complaining about your bad luck with guys. Well a winning lottery ticket has just fallen into your lap. Don't rip it up and throw it away. Cash that baby in for a lifetime's supply of earth-shattering orgasms. Tax free."

And that there was the problem. Dani was right. I *had* been complaining a lot, and George was exactly what I wanted, in all ways but one. There was no "lifetime supply" with guys like George. One night was all I would get. I should go for it anyway. Unless I figured a way out of this visa mess, I wouldn't be in England much longer. I might as well have some fun. He might look and sound like Prince Charming, but he'd be gone in the morning, and I'd be more like Cinderella, which I guess made Ellie and Dani—

"What's going on over there?" Ellie said, pointing to the men who'd been chatting us up earlier.

The three men had surrounded George, and they looked pissed. I moved off my seat to get a better view. I saw the group of women the men had been chatting up. They looked around, trying to get the attention of a manager, but only a few barmaids were on the floor, and they wouldn't do much good.

What had George done? Knowing him, he'd run his mouth and upset the men. His tongue was as strong as all the other muscles in his body, he just didn't know how to control it.

The three guys all looked wired. That trip to the bathroom hadn't been to pee. Women went in packs to powder their nose, and I'd guess these guys had all done the same thing.

"Should we help?" I asked.

"And what help would we be exactly?" Ellie replied. "I suggest we just watch the action."

I protested, but the three of us all walked slowly closer to the scene. We were still twenty yards away, when Whit pushed George from behind. George barely moved in response. Whit pushed him again, harder this time.

Now George reacted. He swung an elbow, and connected with Whit's face, sending him crashing to the floor with a scream of pain. The other two now realized they had to act, but had no idea how. George stood there waiting patiently for them to do something, as if his code of honor wouldn't allow him to make the first move.

Both of the men acted together, but they made a complete hash of it. One guy pushed George, moving him back a yard, while the other tried to punch him. The punch ended up swinging through the air in front of George, who effortlessly grabbed the arm and pulled the puncher towards him.

I couldn't make out what happened in the tangle of legs, but the guy who threw the punch ended up on the floor while the other just ran out of the club as fast as his drug-fueled legs could take him.

"Are you ladies okay?" I heard George ask the women at the table.

"We're fine now, thank you," one of them said, as she eyed George admirably. "I thought we'd be safe from guys like that here, but apparently not."

George looked down at the guy on the floor in front of him. "I don't think they'll be giving you any more trouble."

The guy in front of George looked out for the count, but Whit was moving. "George," I yelled out nervously, as Whit pushed himself to his feet.

"Be there in a minute," he replied.

I rolled my eyes as I watched George lapping up the attention from the ladies. *Men.*

Whit looked dazed from the elbow to the face, but he clearly intended to swing for George.

Fuck it.

I threw my glass—still full of whiskey—and managed to connect with the back of Whit's head. George spun round to see Whit falling back down to the floor, as the glass shattered on the floor.

"Nice throw," George remarked with a smile.

Some bouncers finally came running over ready to take out the trash. "Sorry, Mr. Whittemore. I hope these men didn't bother you."

"Don't worry, Dan. They've been dealt with." He turned back to face me, and smiled. "Now, where were we?"

Chapter Seven

SOPHIA

"You want another whiskey?" George asked.

"I think I'll stick to the Manhattans," I replied.

George ordered our drinks and then we headed over to a table far away from where all the action had gone down. My heart still raced in my chest, but George looked as calm and collected as he had before.

"I don't usually get in fights in bars," George said.

"Why did you this time?"

"Those guys were off their faces. I went over there and some of the things I heard were... not pleasant."

"I can imagine."

"I did ask them to leave first. I even said please."

"I suppose you're used to getting what you want."

George smiled. It was a smile that made me thankful I was sitting down already. "With women, yes," he admitted. "Although some insist on playing hard to get."

"I'm not playing hard to get. I'm just sticking to my end of the bargain."

"So you're only talking to me for the free drinks?" The waitress brought over our drinks at just the right time. I took a long slow sip of my Manhattan, hoping he would forget all about it. He didn't. "Tell you what. You can leave, and I'll still keep the tab open. You're under no obligation to talk to me."

I didn't want to leave. That was half the problem though. I didn't want to leave George now, and I wouldn't want to leave him when he inevitably kicked me out of bed in the morning with nothing more than money for a taxi home.

Besides, if I went back to the girls now, my life wouldn't be worth living.

"I'll stay for a bit," I replied.

"Thought so."

"Why do you want to talk to me anyway?" I asked.

"Why do you think?"

"Same reason as every other guy, I suppose. You want to get laid. What I don't understand, is why single me out? Ellie is prettier than me, and Dani is far easier."

"You're the most beautiful woman in this room, and any other room I've ever been in," George replied, without missing a beat. "And I like a challenge."

I tried to let his words wash over me like the empty compliments they no doubt were. It didn't work. Butterflies fluttered in my stomach, as I looked at this perfect specimen of British muscle, and tried not to let the damp passion between my legs control the words that escaped my mouth.

In some ways, George might even be considered a gentleman. His words made him sound like an arrogant ass, but his actions were at least noble. I'd already seen him step in and help women out twice today, and that hadn't been to get sex. Unless it was all part of a grand plan to get *me* into bed. No, now *I* was the one being arrogant.

I shook my head decisively. "I hope you're not a sore loser, because I'm not going home with you tonight."

We'd both end up losers, but better to lose out in the early stages than suffer the heartbreak of defeat in the final.

"You're very determined to deny yourself pleasure," George said.

"Maybe I don't consider a night with you to be a pleasurable experience."

"Trust me it is. And you know it. I can tell from the way you're sitting."

I was sitting completely normally. I had one leg crossed over the other, and I was facing the person I was talking to. What was suggestive about that?

"You're leaning in to me," George continued when he saw I looked confused. "When you spoke to Whit, you were leaning away. And you're fidgeting."

"Perhaps I'm bored."

"No, you're horny."

"Excuse me," I exclaimed. "You're taking quite the leap there, mister."

George shrugged casually. "Just telling it as I see it. You're sitting there trying to reason with your body, but that won't help. The fire's burning and you can't put it out. You could sit there wafting a fan between your legs and it wouldn't help."

I gasped, but it was more in pleasure than shock. George knew it too. If I overheard a guy talking like this to Ellie, I'd drag her away from him before she could do anything stupid. Why didn't I do the same thing to myself?

Would it really be so bad to have one night with George just to quench my thirst? A few orgasms could at least keep my mind focused for the next couple of weeks.

"Why are you here?" George asked after a few moments of silence.

"Because my friends are complete bitches," I replied. "I should be at home studying."

"No, I mean why are you in the UK?"

"Believe it or not, I thought I might meet some nice men here."

"There's more to it than that," George said. His eyes examined me, as if he were Sherlock Holmes searching for clues. "You're taking a master's degree in a subject you don't seem overly interested in. Plus, you've not come straight from your undergraduate degree. You're a year or two older than most of the other students."

"Thanks," I replied. "Just what every girl wants to hear."

"You're twenty-three," he said, ignoring me. "So you either took a while to graduate the first time, or you took time off."

"I'm a slow learner," I snapped. "I think we've already established that you're cleverer than I am, so... Wait. How do you know I'm twenty-three?"

"I asked the bouncer. Photographic memory that guy. So go on, why are you back at uni, or 'college' as you call it?"

"If you must know, I wasn't going to go to college initially. I was going to be a writer."

"And how did that go?"

"Brilliantly. I'm an international sensation. I just choose to work in a coffee shop for a laugh."

"You're really developing the English knack for sarcasm," George said, smiling again. Did he find everything funny? It was so hard to hate him when he smiled at me like that.

"There were issues," I said softly. "So I went to college. Then there were more issues, so I decided to study in the UK with the goal of staying here after. Except that plan probably won't work out either, because my chances of getting a visa are slim to none.

"So you're running from something? Or someone?"

"It doesn't matter," I said, as images of Stan flooded my mind. "I haven't found what I'm looking for here, and soon I'll have to go home. What's your story? You're clearly rich. Why hang around with girls like me?"

"I told you, you're the most beautiful woman I've—"

"—ever laid eyes on. Yeah, yeah, enough with the bullshit. What's the real reason?"

"Wow, you really get to the point."

"I'm not completely English yet."

For the first time tonight, George looked like he was struggling to find the words. He was weighing up his response, considering whether to tell me the truth, or spin me some bullshit. If he lied, I'd know he was just like every other guy I'd met so far. All I wanted was a bit of honesty.

He shuffled over, so that our bodies were touching, and then reached down and placed a large palm on my upper thigh. I repressed an instinct to flinch away, and instead let the warmth from his fingers travel slowly up to my core.

The fire burned so intently, I felt sure he'd pull his hand away to avoid getting burned. Instead he just squeezed harder as he leaned down to whisper in my ear.

"I want you to come back for sex," George said slowly, but with a steady determination, as if he weighed each word as he spoke it. "I want to give you a night you'll never forget."

Serves me right for wanting honesty I suppose.

"That's not what I want," I lied.

It was what I'd wanted from the moment the airplane had touched down at Heathrow. It was *more* than I'd wanted. Even my wild imagination hadn't created a guy like George in my mind.

Here he was offering it to me on a plate and I didn't know what to do.

"You do want it," George insisted. "Close your eyes, and listen to your body."

I closed my eyes, and once again the music in the background faded away. It was just George and me now. I felt his breath on my neck, as his finger crept a few inches further up my thigh. His nose brushed lightly past my hair, before his soft lips nuzzled against my neck.

I leaned back and let out a light, orgasmic whimper. Then my eyes snapped open as if I'd been violently woken from a dream. We couldn't do this. Not here at least.

"Everything okay?" George asked.

I nodded, and put on my best English accent. "Get your coat, luv. You've pulled."

_*_

We quickly said our goodbyes to a delighted—and slightly jealous looking—Ellie and Dani, before heading outside and straight into a cab.

George insisted on going back to his place, muttering something about not liking the beds in the campus dorms. Fine with me. The walls were thin, and the girls I lived with were judgmental enough as it was.

"Do an English accent again," George whispered in my ear, as his strong hands grabbed hold of my ass in the elevator.

"No," I replied, letting him kiss my neck as he pushed me up against the elevator wall. "That was a one-time thing. Just like this."

George carried me out of the elevator with my legs wrapped around his hips. I heard some old lady mutter "oh my," but I didn't care. I kept my eyes closed until we were inside and I was pressed up against a wall, George's erection pressing up against my sex.

I fumbled with the buttons on his shirt, while he peeled my top off and started kissing the tops of my breasts peeking out above the bra. I gave up trying to undress him and just held on, while his hands and lips devoured my breasts. His cock strained to get out of his pants, as it rubbed against me. The anticipation was enough to have me gushing and on the edge of coming; I hadn't even taken off my skirt yet.

A loud moan escaped my lips like an unexpected hiccup. George looked up at from my breasts and smiled. "I guess it's time we move this into the bedroom."

I nodded, as I felt my face turn red with embarrassment and excitement. "Can we put some music on?" I asked.

"Uh, sure, okay," George replied. "Worried the neighbors will hear you screaming?"

"Force of habit. We have thin walls in the dorms."

"Use the TV. It's connected up to my music library. Don't be long."

George passed me the remote and I flicked the television on. My hand was shaking in anticipation. I wasn't usually nervous having sex. I'd had one night stands before, and I wasn't short on experience with guys. But I'd never met a guy like George before.

Maybe not quite Prince Charming. More like Prince Charming crossed with David Beckham, but perhaps that was what I really wanted after all.

A news channel appeared on the screen, so I quickly tried to change the channel before anything too depressing came on and spoiled the vibe. I changed the channel and then immediately changed it back again.

George's picture was on the screen.

George was on the national news, and he was the lead story.

Chapter Eight

GEORGE

"Oh shit," I moaned as I saw the television screen.

She said I had one more day, God damn it. I should never have trusted a journalist.

"What's going on?" Sophia asked. She didn't take her eyes off the television screen, so I quickly put my shirt and trousers back on. She wasn't going to want to see me half naked after this. She wasn't going to want to see me at all after this.

"Might as well watch and find out," I said. I slumped down on the sofa, and motioned for her to sit next to me. "I'll let you know if any of it's not true."

Sophia didn't sit down, she just stared at me curiously with those damn sexy eyes of hers. "You're not a serial killer are you?"

"Not yet," I replied. "Although there are a few people I wouldn't mind killing right now."

Sophia sat down next to me, but I couldn't help but notice she left a gap of about a foot. So much for tonight's fun.

I hadn't even intended to ask her back here for sex. I had a much more complicated proposal in mind, but my cock had led the discussion. She just looked so damn sexy—so fuckable—in that little skirt and low-cut top. The second I put my hand on her legs it was all over, for both of us. The possible became the inevitable.

I wanted to reach out and touch her leg again to feel that soft skin over firm muscle, and the heat emanating from between her thighs. Probably not a good idea though. She looked freaked out enough as it was. Wasn't every day you found your hookup's face on the national news. I'd had that happen once before, but the news was reporting on Oscar nominations at the time. Boy, that actress had certainly known how to celebrate. Good times.

Sophia turned the volume up as the news studio went to a reporter standing live outside an office building in London. "*The Daily Guardian* has just revealed its cover story for tomorrow, however we only have the bare bones of the story so far."

"What do we know?" the newsroom correspondent asked.

My face stayed on the screen the entire time. They could at least have picked a more flattering photograph, but I suppose that wouldn't sell as many papers. The one they'd used was me coming out of my house after a night spent drinking, shagging, and then drinking again.

"All we know is that the paper is claiming that King Michael did not, in fact, die childless. It appears he had a child two years before his marriage. If true, that child was the heir to the throne and should be King now instead of the current Queen. At the very least, he's a prince."

"Please don't tell me..." Sophia muttered, before trailing off, as the newsroom correspondent asked another question.

"It sounds like the child was illegitimate," she said. "Would an illegitimate child be the heir to the throne?"

"It's complicated, but potentially yes. However, the paper is also claiming that the king married the child's mother briefly as part of a whirlwind romance while he was abroad in America. If that's true, and if the child was conceived during that marriage, we're looking at a new heir to the throne, or possibly even a new monarch."

"No, no, no," Sophia said softly. She hadn't accepted the news yet. That made two of us.

"What do we know about this man?" the woman asked.

"Not a lot. We know that his name is George Whittemore, and he's the son of Mary Whittemore. He has a sister and a nephew."

"Well, whoever this man is, his life will never be the same again after tonight."

Yeah, no shit Sherlock.

I grabbed the remote from a stunned looking Sophia and switched off the television.

"You're a prince," she said quietly. "You're a fucking prince."

"You can call me Prince Charming if you like," I joked. I tried to smile, but it felt forced and awkward. I probably looked more creepy than comforting.

"I… I have to get out of here."

"No," I said quickly, grabbing her arm before she could move. "You can't leave. I mean, you *can* obviously, but you shouldn't. The press might already be out there."

"I'll take my chances."

"Okay then, just stay because I want you to."

"How can you be so calm about this?" she asked. "I don't even understand what's happening. I take it you already knew?"

"Yeah," I said with a nod. "I've known for a while. I thought I had another day or two before the information leaked. Figured I had time to—"

"Screw some more women?"

"Get my affairs in order."

"You're not dying," she snapped. "You're inheriting a fortune. You're going to be... no, I can't even say it. It's too fucking crazy."

You're telling me. A year ago, I was still grieving for my mother's death. Then I found out my father wasn't some drunk my mum had shacked up with for a few months before I was born. He'd been someone entirely different and he'd died recently. People made quite a big fuss about it, what with him being the King and all.

"Just stay the night," I pleaded.

"How will that help? There'll be even more reporters out there in the morning."

"It'll help me. I'll sleep on the sofa."

"You're going to be able to sleep after all this?"

I laughed. "No, I guess not. I'll lay there tossing and turning, while you sleep in my bed."

"You think *I'm* going to be able to sleep after all this?" Sophia sighed loudly, but then laughed. "Ellie is going to love all this. I've hooked up with a Prince after all."

"I really didn't intend for things to go down like this."

"No, I can tell. Your shirt's on inside out, by the way."

"See—I really did just intend to screw you tonight. I was honest."

"You're a noble man, Prince Whittemore. The country is lucky to have you."

I couldn't tell whether she was being sarcastic or not, but I didn't really care. "Just stay the night, please. I want to talk to you about something in the morning."

"I am kind of tired," she said reluctantly. "But you're sleeping on the sofa."

"Sure you don't want to see the crown jewels?" I joked.

"I'm an American. It's probably illegal for me to touch them." She walked over to the bedroom, but stopped in the doorway and turned back to face me. "Goodnight, milord." Sophia gave a mock curtsy, which just meant her skirt rode even further up her backside. God, what I wouldn't give to get a go on that.

Was it too late now? If I could just convince Sophia to go along with my plan, I might not have to become a prince at all.

Sophia was my last hope. It all hinged on her now.

Shame I only met her this morning.

_*_

I'd spent most of the night staring at my phone. Emails, texts, and phone calls flooded in, but the only one I opened was the one from Harry. I'd reached out to him a few weeks ago when I knew the news was going to be made public, but he hadn't believed me. He did now.

Harry was an old friend from college, who'd turned a bad attitude and poor grades into a decent PR career. He was going to come in use over the coming days, weeks, and months.

I sat up on the sofa as I heard the toilet flush from my en-suite, followed by the tap running, and then Sophia walking out of my bedroom. She'd slipped back into the revealing top and short skirt from last night, and looked every bit as sexy, even without the make-up.

"Hi," I said groggily. I'd barely slept, and every time I did, I quickly woke up to nightmares of being crowned king in front of an audience of millions.

"Hi," she replied softly.

At least she didn't sound mad. That was a start.

"Fancy a cup of tea?"

"I'm going to need coffee," she replied. "Or don't you have any?"

"Only instant, I'm afraid."

"Tea it is, then."

I pushed myself up off the sofa and boiled the kettle, while the two of us stood awkwardly in the kitchen. Was I really going to ask her? I barely knew her. But I knew Alisa well enough, and look how that turned out. This was the perfect solution really. I just had to convince Sophia it was worth giving up her life for.

I let the tea brew for a few minutes, then threw the tea bags in the bin and added some milk, before handing it over to Sophia.

"You do make a great cup of tea," she admitted, after taking a sip. "But what is it with you Brits and instant coffee? When you're king, can you declare it illegal?"

"I was hoping you might have forgotten about all that."

"The whole 'you being a prince' thing? No, that's still front and center of my mind right now." Sophia looked around the apartment as if it were somehow different to the place she'd come back to last night. "It's quiet," she remarked. "We haven't been overrun by reporters yet, then?"

"No, thank God. My address hasn't leaked publicly, and I'm using a fake name to rent this place. It's only a matter of time though."

"I haven't heard from the girls yet, which either means they didn't recognize you from that picture, or they haven't seen the news yet. More likely the latter knowing them. They tend to sleep in late after a heavy night."

"I've switched my phone off now. Might as well enjoy my last few moments of peace and quiet."

I sat down on the sofa, but Sophia made a point of sitting on the armchair instead. She crossed her legs, revealing those delicious thighs again. Already I could feel my erection resurfacing in my boxers, reminding me that I hadn't gotten any last night. This situation was stressful enough as it was, without the added pressure from down there.

"You know, some people would think this was good news," Sophia said. "Being a prince might not be a bad life."

"And some people would do anything to shag a prince, and yet you made me sleep on the sofa."

"Fair point. It would have been cool to go home and tell everyone I 'shagged' the future king of England."

"There's still time."

The slight pause before she responded gave me hope, but in the end she shook her head. "Nope. It can't happen. I should never have even come back here."

"I'm glad you did."

"Even though you didn't—how do you say it—get your end away?"

I laughed as Sophia attempted an English accent again. "Oh I do love that accent. And yes, I'm still glad you're here. There's something I wanted to talk to you about actually."

"What's that?" Sophia took a sip of her tea. With hindsight, I probably should have waited until she'd swallowed her drink before popping the question.

"I was wondering whether you would marry me?"

Chapter Nine

SOPHIA

I choked back the mouthful of tea, and laughed nervously. It seemed like an appropriate response. "You... Did you just... What?"

"I want you to marry me," George said sincerely, as if the suggestion weren't just a stupid joke. He sounded deadly serious. "I'll get a ring."

"You think the lack of a ring is the problem here?" I asked. I liked a big diamond as much as the next girl, but it would have to be damn big to blind me to the strangeness of this situation.

"I haven't explained, have I? Shit, sorry, my mind's all over the place right now."

And now so is mine.

Less than twenty-four hours ago, I had been minding my own business working in the café and dreaming about meeting a charming Englishman like the ones I'd seen on television. Then Ellie told me to serve George, and the rest was history. In George's case, it literally would go down in the history books.

I had a story to make me the envy of all my friends. Except I'd never be able to tell them. I couldn't say yes—obviously—and I wasn't about to go spreading tales about the new prince proposing to me. The most exciting thing to ever happen to me, and I'd have to take the story to my grave.

"You're confused," I said to George. "And clearly very sleep-deprived. Perhaps I should leave."

"No," George said quickly. "Give me a chance to explain. I want you to marry me."

"Yeah, I gathered that much when you proposed."

"Right, but not because we love each other or anything. I just want us to get married, and then split up soon after."

My heart sank with disappointment when he admitted he wasn't in love with me. I knew it was stupid; I wasn't in love with him either. It was a gut reaction to hearing the words spoken aloud by a crush. That's all he was. A handsome crush, who was about to be a prince. Or already was a prince. I didn't know how it worked. The details didn't seem important.

"Then why get married?" I asked.

"I need the money. I have an inheritance locked up in a trust and I don't get to claim it until I get married."

"But you're a prince now. You won't need money any more."

"I plan to abdicate. Give up all the titles and the bullshit that goes with it. But I can only do that if I have another source of money."

"Some people work for a living," I said. "Have you thought about that?"

"I need serious money. Millions."

"What for?"

George paused before answering. He liked to think he could read body language, but two could play at that game. He looked embarrassed; whatever the reason, he didn't want to tell me.

"I'm broke," he said eventually. "Nearly, anyway. If I don't get my hands on that inheritance soon, I'm going to be in real trouble."

At least he was being honest with me. That still didn't mean I could go along with this plan. I had far too much going on in my life right now, namely school, paying for school, and all this visa crap hanging over me like—

The visa. If George and I got married, I'd be able to stay in the country easily. I wouldn't have to go back to America. I wouldn't have to face the grief I'd get from my mom, and the looks I'd get from my former friends.

God, this could be so perfect.

But I'd be marrying a prince. I'd had enough drama with my last engagement. I wanted a quiet life now, and I wouldn't get that if we were engaged.

"No," I said firmly. "I'm sorry, but I can't do this. It's too huge."

"I'd pay you. And you could get a visa to stay here permanently. You'd do well out of the arrangement. Trust me, I stand to inherit a *lot* of money."

"I'm not all that keen to prostitute myself out."

"You'd be more like a high-class escort," George replied. I *thought* it was a joke, but you never could tell with the English. "Look, it doesn't have to be anything seedy. You can still go to classes as normal. The only difference being that we would have to live together for a bit."

"Oh, is that all?"

"You know, I really wish you hadn't picked up on the sarcasm thing."

I shook my head again, harder this time, as if I might be able to shake it so hard I could turn back time twenty-four hours.

The proposal had been stupid, but the even stupider thing was I was actually considering it. Living here would be a hell of a lot better than living on campus, and if I got my visa, I'd be able to stay here and never go back to America. I'd sure as hell never have to see Stan again.

But Stan was also the reason I couldn't do this. I couldn't be engaged again. Not now, maybe not ever.

"No. No, I can't. You're a great guy. A really great guy. You'll find someone else to take you up on your offer."

"There's no time. Once I get pulled into the royal bullshit, I'll be trapped. If I'm already married, they might actually let me live a normal life."

"There has to be someone else."

"There was, but it didn't end well. Besides, I don't want just anyone. I want you."

"Why?"

"I like you. You're funny, clever, beautiful, annoying. All attributes I look for in a woman. Look, you don't have to decide now, but I would need an answer soon. Will you think about it?"

I already was thinking about it. Why was I thinking about it? I must be crazy. This was such a bad idea. Even Ellie would say this is too far, and that girl liked to throw caution to the wind.

"I'll think about it," I promised. "But don't get your hopes up."

"Thank you. You would be doing me a huge favor."

"Yeah, no shit. I should get out of here, before the press find out where you live."

"I'll call one of the security guys from downstairs."

A man came up to escort me down to a cab. He needn't have bothered. It was still early, and apparently people liked to sleep in on Saturday mornings because the apartment and the streets were deserted.

I couldn't get engaged again. That was madness. But this wouldn't be a real engagement or a real marriage.

We would just pretend to be a couple for a few months, and then call it off. I did need the money. Maybe not quite as much as George, but it would help me make a fresh start. That's what this entire trip had been about after all. Get my head straight and make a clean break. The visa would be icing on the cake.

I needed to talk to Ellie before I did something stupid. My phone vibrated in my purse. Speak of the devil.

_*_

"Are you going to do it?" Ellie asked.

"No, of course not. That would be crazy. Wouldn't it?"

"Yeah, just a bit."

"Completely," Dani agreed. "Nuts."

They'd said just what I expected, but I was still disappointed to hear it. In the hour it had taken me to get home, have a shower, and get dressed, I'd warmed up to the idea a bit. It didn't have to be such a big deal. People got married and divorced all the time, and the wedding could just be a small civil ceremony. No one would ever have to know the sordid details. No one except Ellie and Dani I suppose. And we wouldn't be the first people in history just to get married for a visa. People did in the US all the time.

"I told him no," I explained.

"What? Why?" Dani asked incredulously.

"Because… I just… weren't you listening to anything I just said?"

"Yeah, I heard. A prince just fucking proposed to you. A lush prince at that."

"Lush is good, right?" I asked Ellie, who often served as my Welsh to American translator. Ellie nodded.

"But you just said it was nuts."

"It is," Dani agreed. "That doesn't mean you shouldn't do it."

I sighed loudly, and suppressed a smile. That was much more what I wanted to hear. "What about you?" I asked Ellie. "Do you think it's 'good crazy' or 'bad crazy?'"

"I usually serve as the voice of reason next to Dani, but..."

"But?"

"But he's a fucking prince," Ellie said, so loudly that my neighbors could probably hear through the thin walls. "I still can't believe I *spoke* to him last night, and that's saying nothing of you spending the evening riding his dick."

"We never had sex," I said. The words slipped out of my mouth before I could stop them. Now I was in trouble.

"You didn't sleep with him?" Dani somehow managed to reach a volume even louder than Ellie. Good job most of the floor was probably sleeping off a hangover.

"Finding out I was kissing a prince came as a bit of a shock believe it or not. What would you have done?"

"I'd have dropped to my knees and had my lips around his dick quicker than you could say 'God save the King.'"

"And I'd have played with his balls," Ellie added helpfully.

"Look," Dani said seriously. "If you don't want to do this, I know one pussy that would be more than happy to ride some royal cock."

"No," I said quickly, as a pang of jealousy hit me in the gut. I couldn't imagine George with Dani or Ellie. I didn't want to think of him with any other women, come to think of it. "It has to be me."

"Why?" Dani asked.

"Uh, something about me being American, and how it will be easier to get out of the royal family side of things."

"This is fate," Ellie said. "You have to do it. And him. Most of all, you have to do him."

'Yep," Dani agreed. "Give him one from us."

"I'm still not doing it," I insisted.

"What are we missing here?" Ellie asked. "You like him right?"

"Yeah, sure. I barely know him, but he seems nice."

"And he's hot," Dani added.

"He's easy on the eyes," I admitted, thinking back to the few glimpses of his chest I'd seen last night through the open buttons. If we got engaged, we wouldn't *have* to sleep together, but I couldn't imagine a scenario where I'd be able to resist. Last night, his hand on my thigh had been enough to get me dripping between the legs. What would I do if I saw him get undressed or come out of the shower with only a towel around his waist?

I'd probably drop to my knees and get my lips around his dick quicker than you could say 'God save the King.'

The physical side definitely wasn't the problem. I just didn't want to be engaged again.

"I never told you girls this," I said, so quietly that the both had to lean in to hear me. "But I was engaged back in the US. Things didn't end well."

Ellie wrapped her arms around me and gave me a hug that I didn't know I needed until I hugged her back. "Sorry sweetie," she whispered. "That must have been horrible."

Yeah, it was. And that was my fault. I certainly didn't deserve anyone's sympathy.

"I'm fine now," I said, once Ellie had let go. "I just don't know if I want to get engaged again."

"Don't treat it like an engagement," Dani said. "You're just hanging out with a hot guy for a few months, and after that you will go your separate ways. And you'll be rich. And famous. You could be the next Kim Kardashian."

"A girl can dream," I said dryly.

Dani was right. We would just be hanging out for a few months, and then we'd split up. Simple, right? Unless I didn't want to split up after a few months.

Unless I fell in love. If that happened, I'd be completely and utterly screwed.

Chapter Ten

GEORGE

I turned my phone to silent, and slipped out of the apartment before I could be surrounded by photographers.

I made a conscious effort to avoid the news, but that was easier said than done. Going online in any way, shape, or form, was basically off the table, and I had to put headphones in to avoid hearing conversations about me.

No one recognized me wearing a large pair of aviators and keeping my head down, but that wouldn't last long. I didn't have a Facebook page, but I had plenty of friends who did. Their photos would soon start popping up, showing me drunk, and with women draped over me.

Then the the sex stories would start. I could just picture the headlines in the tabloids now.

MY NIGHT WITH A PRINCE.
ROYALLY SCREWED.
I SUCKED THE CROWN JEWELS.

I probably deserved the trashy headlines. It was my fault for sleeping with trashy women.

My phone had already collected hundreds of messages, but none of them were from Sophia, so I ignored them. She'd had a few hours to think about it. How long would she need? Most women would jump at the chance to marry a prince, but apparently Sophia was not 'most women.' I knew that already, of course. Sophia was special. Any man would be lucky to have her—even a prince would have to work to earn her affection.

There were other women who would marry me, but I had my heart set on Sophia now. She was the perfect choice.

And she was beautiful. Truly stunning. Was that a good thing? It would certainly make it a lot harder to keep my hands off her for six months, but at least I wouldn't have to fake my desire for her in public. It was definitely better than being a prince and getting some crappy arranged marriage.

I had to avoid that at all costs. If I accepted a position as heir to the throne, my life would be over. I'd have no freedom. It would be all hand-waving, and ribbon-cutting, and whatever other bullshit the royal family did these days.

If I got married and claimed my inheritance, I could avoid all that. Sophia wasn't the only option, but she was the only one I wanted.

I didn't dare call Tabitha in case those bastards at the tabloids were still doing the wiretapping thing, but I did want to see her. As far as I knew, video conferencing was still a fairly secure bet, especially going through a VPN. It was a risk, but it was a risk I had to take. I needed to see Tabitha and Liam. They were the whole reason I was doing this, after all.

I walked to a park where I knew I could get the rare combination of privacy and enough cell phone reception to make a video call. I kept my head down the entire way in case someone recognized me. Did people actually recognize famous faces on the street? I never did, but then I was shit with faces. I hadn't even recognized that actress until we'd finished the deed, and she'd started talking about her Oscar win. I was fairly certain I could bump into Lady Gaga wearing a dress made of meat and I wouldn't recognize her.

I tried calling, but no answer. Of course there was no answer—she was eight hours behind and it was the middle of the night there. My brain wasn't firing on all cylinders.

Still no message from Sophia. Once again, I thought about asking someone else to help me out, but I couldn't imagine it not being Sophia. I wanted to parade her around as my fiancée, and show her off to my friends. I wanted to go on television and tell the world that I was renouncing my claim to the throne because I wanted to spend the rest of my life with Sophia.

Alright, so I'd look like a bit of a tit when we split up six months later, but we'd have fun in the meantime.

My proposal this morning hadn't exactly been the stuff of fairy tales, even if marrying a prince was.

I just had to convince Sophia that this engagement and marriage was the right thing for both of us. She probably needed the money almost as much as I did. Students who worked part-time in coffee shops weren't usually sleeping on mattresses stuffed with £50 notes after all. Not to mention, education in America was expensive, from what I'd heard. She'd have a fuck-tonne of debt that I could clear for her.

And she'd mentioned a visa. Sophia wanted to stay in the country after her studies. If she married me, getting a visa would be a formality. It was a win-win. I just needed to show her that.

_*_

"Oh my God, is that him?"

"Where do I know him from?"

"He sure looks like that prince."

My disguise didn't pass muster close up in a crowded jewelry store. Within seconds, the gossip started, and phones were held in front of faces to record the moment for posterity.

The manager of the story noticed the commotion—and the reason for it—and quickly came over to help.

"Close the store," I demanded.

Might as well make the most of this 'being a prince' thing.

"Yes, sir," the man said, before immediately ushering customers out of the store, and then locking the door. "It's an absolute honor—"

"—to have me in the store. Yes, I'm sure it is. I'm here to buy a ring."

"What type of ring?"

"An engagement ring."

I thought it was only in cartoons when pound signs appeared in people's eyes, but apparently not. At least I'd made one person happy today.

"Absolutely, sir. I mean, Your Highness."

I cringed, and suppressed the urge to vomit. That's why I had to do this. I couldn't handle spending the rest of my life being referred to as "Your Highness."

" 'Sir' will do," I replied. "Now, I'm not sure about all the technical terms, but I want something big and shiny. Something I can't look directly at for too long without going blind."

"Yes, sir. Right this way."

The man disappeared into the back room and came out with a rock the size of Gibraltar.

"Oh yes, that will do nicely."

Chapter Eleven

SOPHIA

There was nothing like serving coffee all day to bring a princess down to earth.

"God damn it," I cursed, as the cappuccino machine spluttered and sprayed boiling hot water all over my hands. The machine should have been thrown out years ago.

"I don't know why you're even here," Ellie said, as she grabbed me by the wrist and shoved my hand under cold running water. "You're going to be rich soon. This is no place for the fiancée of a prince."

"Keep your voice down," I whispered.

Every woman in the café was already talking about the new prince, especially now it had been discovered that he lived locally. I'd overheard a few students saying they'd spent the night with him, but I didn't know whether to believe them. I didn't *want* to believe them, but I knew the odds weren't exactly in my favor on that one.

George had never claimed to be wholesome and innocent, but he'd also made me feel special. Unique. Knowing he'd slept with half the girls at my college didn't help, but I wasn't exactly innocent either. If I did go ahead with this crazy plan, there'd be a few guys here bragging about how they'd screwed a princess.

That was a thought I had to get out of my head immediately. I wasn't a princess, and even if I became one, it would be a fleeting title. I'd lose it again when George and I went through the inevitable divorce.

At least we would actually get married. That was one step further than my last engagement.

"I'm just saying," Ellie continued, "that you should be at home thinking this decision over. Then, when you finally come to your senses and decide to marry him, you won't ever have to work here again. Although, come to think of it, I would like you to work out your notice so that I'm not left in the lurch."

"I'm sure I can send in a servant to work my shift," I joked. "Anyway, I don't think I can go through with this. It's going to end badly; I just know it."

"I don't know how you can say no to him. Literally. I don't know if it's physically possible to say no to a man like that. The other day, I closed my eyes and imagined him proposing to me. When I opened my eyes, my legs were wide open."

I laughed at Ellie's joke, but from the look on her face she was being deadly serious.

My hand still stung, but I pulled it away from the water and dried it off with a towel. There was already a line forming at the counter, and I needed to keep my mind occupied. Conversations like this weren't helping.

A man coughed loudly behind me trying to get my attention. That made my blood boil more than a broken cappuccino machine. Weren't the English supposed to be good at waiting in line? I thought it was a national pastime. It was more exciting than cricket at least.

"Just a minute," I yelled out. Impatient prick.

I paused while putting the finishing touches to the coffee that had led to me getting a burned hand. The atmosphere in here had changed. The sound of fingers moving furiously over keyboards had disappeared, replaced by whispered conversations.

When I turned around, the first thing I saw was a room full of people all pulling out their phones and holding them up in the air. Then I noticed what the phones were all pointed towards.

George was standing at the front of the line just like he had been yesterday. Except now he had been outed as a prince.

"Hi," he said casually. He appeared to be blissfully unaware of the attention he was getting. Either that or he didn't care.

"Hi."

"Can we talk?"

This was it. Decision time.

The gossip in the café ramped up a level as people began speculating why a prince might want to talk to the American girl who worked in the university coffee shop.

"Let's go somewhere private," I suggested.

"I don't think we're going to get any privacy right now," George said. "And I don't care."

"You want an answer?"

"Yes. But I also want the opportunity to ask the question again. Properly this time."

George dropped to one knee, and pulled a small box out of his pocket. The collective gasp from the customers could have been heard the next town over. Regardless of what happened next, this moment would be played on televisions and websites the world over. I was already famous. Even if I said no, my life would never be the same again.

"Sophia Simpkins," George said determinedly. "Will you do me the honor of becoming my wife?"

I was speechless. Even more surprisingly, so was Ellie. I still didn't have an answer, and now I had no more time to think about it. I couldn't do this, could I?

This is insane.
Absolutely batshit crazy.
I should run away and never look back.
I should—
George opened the box.
Holy shit, that's a big rock.

_*_

"People are going to assume we're shagging."

"Would you like me to make some satisfied noises?" I asked. "There are bound to be people outside my room trying to get the scoop. Wouldn't want you to look bad."

"No, it's alright. I'm sure there are enough kiss and tell stories doing the rounds about me by now. The whole world probably knows what I'm capable of in bed."

"What happens next?" I asked, quickly changing the subject.

"We go out in public together a few times to make it convincing, and then get married."

"Who are we trying to convince?"

"The trustees of the trust set up by my biological father. They won't ask too many questions, but I'd like to make sure. They'll hand over the money, then we'll get divorced, and live happily ever after."

"Just like a fairytale."

George turned serious and took hold of my hand, leading me over to the sofa. I sat down next to him and this time our legs touched. My mind flashed back to last night in the club when his hand had touched my leg. How stupid was it that brushing up against my fiancé's leg was enough to get me excited?

"I know I joke about this, but I do appreciate what you're doing. I promise I'll make it worth your while."

"I know you will."

"We'll have to live together, but I can sleep on the sofa."

I nodded, but we both knew it wouldn't be as simple as that. We'd almost slept together after a few drinks in a club; how would we resist each other if we lived in the same house?

"My mom's going to kill me," I said. "Seriously, she is going to be pissed."

"I can charm your mother, don't you worry."

"It's not as simple as that. She won't be happy about me getting married. Not after the last time."

"You've been married before?"

The story was probably all over the internet by now, and it wouldn't be flattering.

"No," I said. "I nearly got married. I called off the engagement."

"Oh, well that's okay. Nothing to worry about."

"When I say 'I called off the engagement' I mean I ran away on the day of the wedding."

"Ah."

"Yeah. Probably should have mentioned that I guess."

A look of intense thought stretched across George's face, but then he relaxed into one of his mesmerizing smiles. One of the smiles that melted my heart. No man had ever looked at me like that before. Not even Stan.

"People will think we're made for each other," George said. "I've got a reputation for... well, for appreciating the female form. And you've abandoned a guy at the alter. We're two long lost souls, afraid of commitment until we found each other."

"You almost make this sound romantic."

"It could be, if you want it to be."

"One step at a time, tiger, one step at a time."

Chapter Twelve

GEORGE

This might not have been a good idea.

I wanted to introduce my new fiancée to the country as quickly as possible. It was a nice day, so Sophia suggested we go to York Castle and look around because "we don't have all that many castles in America."

It somehow never occurred to me that walking around a castle when you've just been announced as heir to the throne might not be the best idea. I looked like I was getting ready to rule the country, when all I wanted to do was claim my inheritance and run. This was the sort of thing I should have run by Harry first.

"Can I touch it?" Sophia asked.

"We should probably wait until we have some privacy, but sure, you can cop a feel if you like."

Sophia pursed her lips in a way that made me desperate to lean over and kiss her. I'd only kissed her on the cheek so far today, and it was driving me crazy.

"I meant the rocks," she replied. "Are we allowed to touch them?"

"Oh, yeah sure. It's not a museum."

We had to keep our conversations to a whisper to avoid being overheard. English Heritage had agreed to grant us a private visit, but there was always a member of staff in earshot.

"It just feels weird to touch something so old." She reached out and placed her hand against what was left of the castle wall. According to the sign we were standing in what would have been a kitchen.

"I guess we take it for granted," I replied. "I forget you guys don't have any history."

"We have plenty of history thank you very much."

"Like what?"

"Well, there's the small matter of that little war where we kicked your asses out of the country two hundred and fifty years ago."

"Two hundred and fifty years? Please, that's not history. In England, we refer to that as 'current events.' History is the dark ages, the crusades, the reformation, kings and... other stuff."

"You're going to be in the—"

"Don't say it," I interrupted. "I'm not going to be in history books, and I'm not going to be taught in schools. This will all be over in six months, and then everyone will go back to normal."

"I still don't understand why you don't want to be a prince," Sophia said. "You'd get to wear a crown one day. You'd look good in a crown; assuming you can find one to fit your head."

"If you like me in a crown, I'll wear one. But let's keep the dress up to the bedroom."

Sophia smiled, and looked away, pretending to read an information sign that I knew she'd already read. I'd spent last night on the sofa, and we were still tip-toeing around the whole 'sex' thing. That didn't stop me getting a stonking great big erection when she came out to get a glass of water wearing only a pair of tight cotton shorts and a strappy top that had me struggling to look at anything other than her pert nipples.

"Do you not like the royal family?" Sophia asked. "They seem nice enough."

"I don't know them. Not yet. I'm sure they're lovely people, but that doesn't matter. I don't want their lifestyle. I just want to get my money and run."

Sophia struggled to control her hair, as a bitter wind blew through the open castle walls. What would it have been like living here hundreds of years ago? Even with fires blazing, it would have been difficult to keep warm during the winter when temperatures dipped below freezing. I suppose it helped when you had someone to snuggle up to.

I wrapped an arm around Sophia's shoulder, brushed the hair out of her face, and kissed her gently on her cold forehead. She put both arms around me and hugged me tightly. I didn't look behind me, but I knew some of the staff would be taking pictures of this moment. I didn't care; it looked good for the cameras. The trustees would be completely convinced.

I know I am.

_*_

The manager of the gift shop made a huge fuss over us the second we walked through the door. I hated it. If this was what being a prince was like, then I knew I was making the correct decision.

"If there is anything I can do for you both, anything at all, then just let me know," the manager said before stepping to the back of the store to give us some semblance of privacy.

"He's still watching us," Sophia said. "Maybe he thinks we're going to steal something."

"You're American. He's probably worried this is the prelude to an invasion."

"Or maybe he thinks you might want assistance, but you'll never ask for it because the English are so afraid to speak up."

"Or he's waiting for you to start a loud conversation on your phone, or pull out a selfie stick."

"Hey," Sophia said loudly. "I do not own a selfie stick. Although they do look useful."

"Somehow I don't think we'll ever need help getting our picture taken."

"Oh my God," Sophia exclaimed loudly. She couldn't have sounded more American if she'd have put her hand on her chest and started singing the national anthem. "They have mugs."

"Of course they have mugs. It's a gift shop."

"No, I mean they have mugs of you. Look."

Now I just wanted to vomit. It wasn't even a flattering picture. Weren't there any photos of me were I wasn't drunk or hungover? "How did they even get these mugs made so quickly?"

"They aren't exactly the best quality. I suppose they'll do some for the royal wedding as well."

"That's why we're going to have a private wedding."

Sophia put down the mug and grabbed some sweets. "Let's get this fudge and then go sit outside again."

"You look cold," I remarked, staring at her arms and chest. "Grab a jumper as well." Probably shouldn't have said that; why was I encouraging her to cover up?

We stood at the top of the castle with a view overlooking the town and shared the bag of fudge between us. We'd be in range of anyone with a half-decent zoom lens now, but the pictures couldn't be any worse than the ones they already had of me. At least I wasn't drunk.

Sophie slipped on the jumper and lifted up the hood to stop her hair blowing everywhere. Had a princess ever been photographed in a hoodie before? Maybe. Had a princess ever been photographed looking so beautiful? Definitely not.

I'd never been so captivated by a woman showing so little skin. All I could see was her hands and face. Both were red with the cold, and she continually had to sweep the hair from her eyes.

"Do you think we've accomplished our mission for the day?" Sophia asked.

"Yeah, I think so. Why? Do you want to go home?"

"No, let's stay here for a bit. The view's nice."

"It certainly is," I agreed.

Sophia rested her head on my shoulder, as she reached her hand into the bag for another piece of fudge. The ring sparkled from the rays of the setting sun. It suited her.

"What do you want to do tomorrow?" Sophia asked.

"We don't have to spend every day together," I replied. "Not if you don't want to."

"I'm not bored of you yet. We can hang out if you like."

"I would like that. How about we stay in and watch The Tudors on Netflix? I want you to find out what happens when Queens step out of line."

"Oh please. You forget there's been a power shift since the sixteenth century dear."

"Kings still rule over Queens."

"Yes, but I'm American, remember? Try to behead me and we'll kick your ass so hard you'll be driving on the right hand side of the road, and singing the American national anthem before soccer games."

"We'll see about—" I paused as my phone vibrated in my pocket. We hadn't had any signal in last few hours, so I'd been left alone, but I guess we'd found a few bars of reception. Lucky me.

"Aren't you going to answer it?" Sophia asked.

"I suppose I need to start telling people to piss off at some point. I really should make that my answerphone message."

I answered the call, but I did little more than say yes 'four' times and then hang up.

"Who was it?"

"Change of plans for tomorrow. You need to go shopping to buy a dress."

"Oh. Well, if you insist. Where are we going?"

"To the registry office. The wedding's been booked. We're getting married."

Chapter Thirteen

SOPHIA

"What the hell are those things on your face?" Dani asked.

"They're sunglasses."

"They're a little... big," Ellie added delicately.

"I need them to cover my face so that no one will recognize me," I explained.

"Well it's working," Dani said. "I did not for one minute think you looked like a future princess."

"Keep your voice down," I pleaded. "This is an incognito shopping trip. I just need to buy a dress and then we can leave."

"Sounds fun," Ellie said dryly. Despite what George seemed to think, I hadn't quite gotten the hang of English sarcasm yet, so I had no idea whether Ellie was excited or not.

"You can each get a dress too. George's treat."

"Oh, now it sounds fun," Ellie exclaimed.

Okay, she was being sarcastic before then.

"Good. I don't know where the best shops are, so I'll need you ladies to lead the way. Got any places in mind?"

"How formal is the event?" Dani asked. "Next and Topshop do decent enough dresses that can pass as formal at a push."

"It's for a small gathering in town. You're both invited."

"And who will be at this small gathering?" Ellie asked.

"Just the three of us and George. And a minister."

Ellie and Dani looked at each and then back at me. "You're getting married?" Dani yelled.

"That's generally what happens after an engagement."

"Yes, but I didn't know it would happen so soon."

"What you're saying," Ellie broke in, "is that you need a dress for a wedding."

"Yep."

"Your own wedding?"

"Yep."

"So you need a wedding dress," Ellie concluded.

"I guess so," I agreed. "But it doesn't have to be anything too fancy. I'm not wearing white. I just want a normal dress."

"I don't think Topshop is going to cut it," Dani said. "There's a little boutique place in the mall that doesn't have a price tag on anything. Let's start there."

I kept my "bitch glasses" on, as Dani called them, while we walked through the mall to a small store at the back which was mercifully quiet. They also sold wedding dresses, but there were no excited brides to be in here yet.

Except me.

The lady running the store measured me, and then went to a back room to bring out some styles for me to try. She didn't comment on the glasses, but I decided to take them off. I probably looked like a woman who'd been beaten, and that was very much not the vibe I wanted to give off.

"We saw the pictures of you online," Ellie said.

"Oh God, I haven't even looked. What are they like?"

"Romantic," Ellie replied. "There are some of you holding hands while walking around the ruins of a castle, and there's a great one where he kisses you on the forehead."

"Don't forget the one of them snuggling up at the top of the castle and looking out at the view," Dani added.

"Good," I said. "We're supposed to look convincing."

"Oh you looked convincing all right," Ellie said. "I know I'm convinced."

"Me too."

"Alright, ladies. What's your point?"

"Our point is," Dani said, in typically loud fashion, "you like him. And he likes you."

"Obviously we like each other," I said. "I wouldn't do this with someone I hated."

"You nearly slept together," Ellie helpfully pointed out.

"*Nearly* being the operative word."

"So you still haven't bumped uglies?" Dani asked.

"No, and we're not going to."

The manager came back to save me from further grilling, and she hung up three dresses in a fitting room for me. All the dresses looked more expensive than my entire wardrobe put together. George was going to need that inheritance money to pay his credit card bill.

"Can you measure my friends too, please?" I said to the manager. "They are getting a dress each as well."

"Of course, Ma'am."

"I'd like one a little more revealing at the front," Ellie said.

"And just make mine straight up slutty," Dani said. "The sort of thing you wouldn't let your daughter leave the house in. Oh, and make sure it's a dark color. I have this unfortunate habit of getting grass stains on my dresses."

"I'm sure I can come up with something," the lady said, before disappearing again.

I ruled the first dress out before even trying it on. Red seemed too erotic for a wedding. The second dress fit perfectly, and was certainly modest enough for a low-key ceremony. It was also boring. I didn't want to embarrass myself at the altar, but I also had a fiancé to keep interested.

The third dress was light green and trailed down below my knees, but with some ruched styling that revealed plenty of my right thigh. It was sexy; perhaps a little too sexy.

"Can you tie me up?" I yelled, as I stepped out of the fitting room in the third dress, holding the straps that needed to be tied around the back of my neck.

Ellie and Dani stared at me, but made no effort to help.

"What?" I looked down to make sure I didn't have a nipple showing. "Can I get some help?"

Ellie shook her head and ran over to tie me up. "Sorry, honey. I just can't believe how perfect you look."

"If you dare say I look fit for a prince, I won't be held responsible for my actions."

"She's right," Dani said. "You look stunning. George won't be able to keep his hands off you."

My heart skipped a beat, as I imagined George reaching behind my neck and undoing the strap, before watching my dress fall to the floor.

"I should try on some more," I said quickly. "This might not be the right one."

It might be too *perfect.*

"You're buying that dress," Ellie insisted. "And I very much suggest you buy some sexy undies to go with it, because you won't be sleeping alone once George sees you in that."

"Screw that, you should go commando," Dani said. "You can't beat that feeling."

"I can't get married without any panties on."

George would love it though. He'd be drooling all day. Then the second we were alone, he'd have me up against the wall, devouring me with his lips like he had done a few nights ago. This time he wouldn't stop at my nipples.

"I guess I could buy this one," I said with feigned reluctance. "Now you two get your dresses sorted out."

"Shall we go to Ann Summers after for some panties?" Ellie asked.

"No, I'm good."

Perhaps I didn't need underwear after all. I never did like a visible panty line.

Chapter Fourteen

GEORGE

The venue deserved a proper wedding, not a wedding of convenience. It might only be a registry hall, but the building was old and beautiful. Yorkshire had history everywhere you looked, so I'd always walked past this building without giving it a second thought. However, when you truly stopped and looked, the beauty was impossible to miss. White marble pillars adorned the entrance, and the small set of steps leading up to the old door carried a surprising amount of grandeur.

Inside, the building was cramped, and the furniture was cheap, but the art on the walls, and the pictures of couples married hundreds of years ago, all lent a weight of authenticity.

Despite all that, we were able to squeeze in a wedding ceremony at short notice. People really didn't appreciate what was right on their own doorstep.

"How do I look?"

I spun around and came face-to-face with the blushing bride.

Speaking of things that deserve better than a wedding of convenience.

Given the circumstances of the wedding, Sophia and I had agreed to forego all the formalities and traditions, but once she'd brought Ellie and Dani in on the plan, that all went out the window.

The girls insisted I not see Sophia on the morning of the wedding—which was quite easy to manage given that we weren't sleeping together—and I hadn't been allowed to see the dress.

Sophia had picked out a light green dress with a ruched bottom and sweetheart cut at the top. She looked more like a prom queen than a bride, but that was just fine with me. That was one American tradition I could definitely get behind.

"You look radiant," I replied.

"That's how you describe a pregnant woman."

"Okay, then you're glowing."

"Also how you describe a pregnant woman. Do I look fat in this?"

"You look stunning," I insisted. I looked down at the silver chain necklace supporting an emerald gem that hung tantalizingly just above her breasts.

"Eyes up, mister."

"Just admiring the necklace."

"Actually, with the amount of effort it took to get my tits into this thing, you might as well stare at them."

"Well, if you insist."

The one problem with a registry office wedding was that you basically had to wait in line. It was already midday—our allocated start time—but apparently weddings were like doctor's appointments. You had to arrive on time even though the doctor was always running three appointments behind.

This didn't feel right. I'd always thought of weddings as being pointless, and Sophia and I had always talked about this as being just a legal arrangement. Which it was. In theory.

However, it was hard to think about the theory when I had the most beautiful woman I'd ever laid eyes on standing next to me. She can't have ever imagined this would be how her wedding day went down. Just because I hated the damn things, didn't mean I was completely oblivious to the fantasy of the perfect wedding.

Sophia had two friends with her, but no family members. She wore a lovely dress, but it wasn't white. The location was great, but she deserved a large church or cathedral. We could have had a grand royal wedding if we wanted to. Streets would have been closed, and the country would have had the day off work. Instead, we were waiting in the hallway of a registry office.

Had I rushed her into the decision? My proposal at the coffee shop had been a little abrupt, but she'd been leaning towards saying yes anyway. Plus, this benefited both of us. Sophia had confessed that she wanted a visa. This way she got to stay in the country after her degree, and I got to inherit a small fortune.

But still…

"It's not too late to back out," I whispered in Sophia's ear. "I can take the blame if you want."

"Are you having second thoughts?"

"No, not at all. But if you are… well, I just don't want you too feel under any pressure to do this."

"There's no pressure. It's just a piece of paper. My life won't be any different tomorrow."

"Actually, you'll be a princess and potentially a future Queen of England."

"Oh yeah."

"Small change."

"I can live with it."

I couldn't stop a smile from spreading across my face. If anyone saw us, we would look like a genuine couple in love and ready to spend the rest of their lives together.

Sophia started fiddling with her breasts, so I looked over her shoulder and caught Ellie's eye. Ellie had been cool about this entire thing. She was close to Sophia, but she wasn't a crazy, overprotective friend. That might have lulled me into a false sense of security, because looking at Ellie now, I knew that if I hurt Sophia there would be hell to pay. I also knew I would never do that, and not because I was scared of Ellie. Well, not *just* because I was scared of Ellie.

The staircase creaked as a couple walked down the stairs hand in hand, followed by a flock of bridesmaids, men in suits, and women hidden under big hats. They were all so caught up in the wedding that they walked right past us and out of the door without so much as a glance in our direction. That was how it should be.

A few minutes later, our minister walked halfway down the stairs and called out for us to follow him.

"Here goes," I said to Sophia, trying my best to give a reassuring smile.

"Hang on," Ellie yelled out. "George, you need to go up first, and then we need to walk behind Sophia and hold up her train."

"I don't have a train," Sophia argued. "You're just going to be holding up my skirt and getting an eyeful of my ass."

"We're doing it anyway," Ellie insisted, as her and Dani got in position.

"I think I'd like to stand behind her as well," I suggested. "Sounds like there's a great view."

"Get up those stairs, George," Dani snapped.

"Christ, I knew married life would involve being bossed around, but I'd assumed that would be coming from the missus."

I jogged up the stairs and introduced myself to the minister.

"Oh wow," he said, when he shook my hand. "I'd seen the names on the calendar, but I assumed someone was playing a joke. It's really you."

"It's really me."

"Didn't think I'd ever conduct a royal wedding."

"Didn't think I'd ever be in one."

Our conversation ended with the ear-splitting noise of a northern girl and a welsh girl screeching "here comes the bride" at the tops of their already loud voices.

"You're definitely going to remember this one," I said to the registrar, who looked like he was on the verge of putting his hands over his ears.

He'd remember it, and so would I. The top floor of the building was a large open space which had probably once been a large attic, but now had a small archway and a modest amount of chairs for guests. Technically, we could have just sat down at a table, said a few words and signed the paperwork, but Ellie had insisted we at least make it look vaguely like a real wedding. Neither Sophia nor I had put up much of a fight. That still surprised me.

I blocked out the noise—I mean singing—and focused on Sophia as she appeared at the top of the stairs and walked towards me. Regardless of my feelings for marriage, I couldn't help but be moved at the sight of her walking slowly in that dress with Ellie and Dani picking up the rear.

It's not real, I reminded myself. *It's a legal requirement, and it means nothing.*

So why was I nervous? Grooms were supposed to be nervous on their wedding days, but that was because they were in love. And stupid. The two usually went hand in hand.

"Please join hands," the registrar said. I took Sophia's hands in mine. It had been many years since the act of holding hands had ever been a thing to set my heart racing, but that's what was happening now. "George, we'll start with you. Please repeat after me."

Chapter Fifteen

SOPHIA

It was all over in three minutes. A bit like the night I lost my virginity, except not as painful and my friends hadn't been watching that night. I hoped not, anyway.

"So that's it?" I asked. "We're married?"

"Not quite," the registrar explained. "You still need to sign a paper to make it all legal."

He ushered us over to a table in the corner where the paperwork lay out ready for us to sign. This bit scared me more than the ceremony. Ellie and Dani putting on a fuss had been so over-the-top for the occasion, that I'd found the entire thing more comical than serious. Until I'd reached the altar, at least.

The second George took his hands in mine, my heart started fluttering wildly and inconsistently, and I suddenly felt rather nauseous. I told myself it wasn't real again and again, but when I'd had to repeat the vows to George, they'd sounded real enough.

But then it had all ended. Now there was just the simple matter of committing fraud as the first step towards getting a visa to live in England. None of this seemed to bother Ellie and Dani, who happily signed the document as witnesses to this whole affair.

"Okay, congratulations," the registrar said. "You are now husband and wife."

"Photo time," Ellie screamed loudly. "Get together you two. Sophia, kiss him on the cheek."

I pressed my lips up to George's cheek, but made sure not to actually make a kissing motion. If there was no noise it wasn't a real kiss.

"George, do the same to Sophia."

George placed his lips on my cheek, but there was definitely a noise this time.

"Come on," Dani pleaded. "You're not cousins. Look like you care."

George squeezed up close to me and placed his hand on my thigh. It would have been an innocent enough gesture between husband and wife, but I felt like he shouldn't be touching me that way in public. Contact from George sent a heat coursing through my body, and made me want to be somewhere private. No doubt I'd be bright red in this photo.

Our lips touched and we held the pose for five seconds while Ellie and Dani took photos. This time it was definitely a kiss.

Ten minutes ago, I'd been a single lady—now I was officially married to a man who would soon be recognized as a prince. That made me a woman about to be confirmed as a princess. It was a lot to take in for an American girl from a small town in California.

George and I walked down the stairs hand-in-hand, and headed straight to a small park across the street. I stuck to the path because my heels would be instantly lost in the grass, and I'd end up on my ass in no time at all. Going commando, that could be a big problem.

"I need to go make a quick call," George said. "See you soon, wifey." He smiled awkwardly and kissed me on the cheek, before disappearing around the corner.

"I can't believe someone's made an honest woman out of you," Ellie joked.

"I don't know if 'honest' is the best word to use, given the circumstances."

"Good point. But I'm still jealous."

"There's nothing to be jealous about," I insisted. "We'll be divorced in six months."

"I hope you're at least going to enjoy your wedding night," Dani said. "You can't let a man like that go to waste. I don't know about the whole fraudulent visa thing, but I know that not screwing George would be criminal."

"She's right," Ellie added. "Besides, isn't it a legal requirement to consummate the marriage?"

"I very much doubt it. Look, I didn't mind you making a big deal of the wedding, but now we need to get back to normality. I'm still a student with coursework to complete."

"Sorry, but it doesn't work like that," Dani said. "You're going to be a public figure. There's no way you can just go back to living a normal life now. There will be parties, fundraisers, art galleries to open, and all that other bullshit."

"You make being a princess sound difficult," Ellie said.

"It is," Dani replied. "I wouldn't do it. I enjoy my freedom too much. I want to be able to shag who I want, when I want. I definitely don't want the press recording my every move. Mind you, for George I would be tempted."

"That's why George doesn't want to become a prince," I pointed out. "He enjoys his freedom." Which for him, meant screwing as many women as possible. For some reason, I couldn't get all that excited about helping him achieve that particular goal.

"You'll still have freedom," Ellie said. "It's not like it was in the olden days. Royals are just celebrities, really. Sure, it's a bitch to have no privacy, but you're also rich and famous. That has to be good."

"You're forgetting that this is temporary. It'll be over before you know it."

"All the more reason to enjoy those six months of fame. Speaking of which, when are you going to come out as a married couple? You won't be able to keep this secret for long. Someone's going to tip off the press."

"I think that's what George is discussing now with his friend. I guess this means I'm going to have to tell my mom soon."

"You haven't told your Mom?" Ellie screeched. "My God, she's going to go mad."

"Yep, probably. We haven't spoken that much lately. She was furious at me for walking out on the wedding. The last one. There was lots of screaming and yelling, and we never really made up. We weren't that close to begin with."

"That sucks," Dani said.

Dani and her mom were like sisters. Just a few days after I'd met Dani, I'd overheard her having a really explicit conversation about a couple of guys she'd slept with in the last month. I turned red just listening to the details, but I practically keeled over in shock when she said "bye, Mom" at the end.

Mom and I were nowhere near that close, and I didn't have any siblings. After the incident with Stan, I didn't have many friends either—not ones I could count on anyway. Ellie and Dani more than made up for it though. Better to have two great friends than ten average ones.

"Are you both heading back to school now?" I asked the girls.

"It's university, not school," Ellie corrected. "You make us sound like sixteen year olds."

"I still don't understand the difference, but whatever."

"I guess we *should* head back," Ellie said. "I'm getting hungry. Turns out being maid of honor is enough to work up an appetite."

"George suggested we all get lunch together if you fancy it?"

"We could go to the pub on the corner?" Dani suggested. "They do a great roast."

"The cocktail selection sucks though," Ellie pointed out.

"True."

"It's only just midday," I pointed out. "Isn't it a bit early for cocktails?"

Ellie and Dani looked at each other and shook their heads. "You really haven't adapted to the British way of life yet, have you?" Ellie asked. "Pubs open at eleven in the morning for a reason."

"Alright," I said, holding up my hands. "But let's go somewhere nice. George is paying."

"Oh, well why didn't you say so," Dani replied. "I know just the place."

"I thought you might. I'll go hurry George up."

George had disappeared from sight, but he couldn't have gone far. I hobbled over as quickly as I could in my high heels, and saw him standing on the corner of the park with his back to me.

I slowed to a walk and called out his name, but he didn't hear me. He sounded like he was finishing up his conversation anyway.

"Let me know what she says," George said to the person on the other end of the phone. "Good news, or bad news, I want to know."

I stood back to let him end the call. It was a bit early to be a nagging wife demanding all his time and attention.

He muttered something else incomprehensible into the phone, and then a few more words that I did catch.

"Okay, speak to you soon, Tabitha. Love you. Bye."

Chapter Sixteen

GEORGE

The news of our marriage had leaked out before we'd even left the pub after lunch. Ellie and Dani had jumped in a taxi to get back to university, but Sophia and I fled home where—despite me offering—we did not get to consummate the marriage.

Sophia attempted to go to class once, but the media chaos stopped her even getting close to the lecture hall. After that, the university doubled down on security, but Sophia decided to take some time off from her studies. She'd catch up easily enough.

The media eventually moved on from the shock of my existence, and started debating what the hell was going to happen to the order of succession. The consensus was that the current royal family were fucked. My claim was valid, and I could easily prove it with a DNA test.

Right now, there was a Queen on the throne likely quite concerned about the need to move house soon, and a Prince and Princess watching their future disappear down the drain. They had every reason to hate me, and yet for some reason we got an invitation to dinner at Clarence House.

I would have declined, but Sophia got hold of the invitation and insisted we attend. At least it was another excuse to see her in a formal dress again. That was worth a night spent talking to the royals I was about to usurp.

_*_

If I were ever King, the first thing I'd do is cut down on the eleven layers of security it took to enter a building. It seemed fucking rude in my book to invite someone to your house and then treat them like criminals on the way in.

Not to mention, one of the guards had the nerve to put his hands on Sophia. I hadn't even done that yet. Not recently, anyway.

If the ride from the airport had taken one minute longer, I wouldn't have been responsible for my actions. The dark blue silk clung to her body enough that I could picture her completely naked. The dress was nearly entirely backless, revealing a part of her I hadn't seen yet, but as usual, it was the legs that had me captivated.

Had I always been a leg man? I certainly was where Sophia was concerned. Perhaps standing all day for work was a good way to keep the legs toned. It certainly hadn't done her any harm.

The dinner turned out to be a rather intimate affair, but that was just fine with me. Just Prince Stuart and his younger sister, Princess Mary. Plus about twenty servants.

"I'm afraid Mother couldn't make it,' Stuart said, referring to the Queen. "Well, that's not quite true. She could, but she thought it would be inappropriate to meet at this stage."

"No problem," I replied. As much as I liked to play it cool, meeting the Prince and Princess had set off a few butterflies in my stomach. Meeting the Queen would have been something else entirely.

I probably shouldn't be here anyway, but Sophia and I agreed it would be best to keep the appointment.

We wanted to look like a normal couple for the time being, and normal couples wouldn't turn down trips to meet the royal family. Besides, if my plan went wrong, I might still need to play the part of a prince for a bit. That thought held less appeal with each passing minute.

We all sat down at a table that was far too large for just the four of us. A servant appeared over my shoulder to pour wine. Not exactly my drink of choice, but perhaps it was a little early for whiskey.

"It's lovely to meet you," Mary said.

"Same," I replied briefly.

"I love your dress," Sophia said enthusiastically. I was used to American accents, but tonight her accent stood out a mile in a place where even the servants spoke the Queen's English. It just made me want her even more.

"Thank you," Mary replied. "Yours is absolutely divine. Mother would never let me wear something so risqué."

"To be honest, neither would mine," Sophia admitted. "She'll have a fit when she sees me on television later."

Mary immediately warmed to Sophia, although she looked like she hadn't spoken to a 'normal' person in years. When Mary found out Sophia was from California, she asked her if she'd "bumped into" any celebrities. I opened my mouth to point out that California was actually bigger than the UK; you didn't just 'bump into' celebrities on a regular basis. I decided against it. I'd already displaced her in line for the throne; no need to make her look stupid as well.

"I'd love to meet Jennifer Lawrence," Sophia admitted, after Mary had asked her what the Oscars were like. "I suppose I'll be able to do that now."

"I've met her," I said, the words slipping out before my brain could stop them.

"When?" Sophia asked.

"Uh, nevermind. Story for another time perhaps."

Butlers came out and served us the first course to save me any further questions on that topic.

"Start from the outside in," I whispered to Sophia, who looked confused by all the cutlery choices.

"How do you know all this stuff?" she asked.

"Must be in the genes."

Stuart must have overheard because he suddenly turned red and looked distinctly uncomfortable. He'd been calm all evening, but it wouldn't have escaped his notice that I stood to push him down the pecking order.

"We should probably deal with the large elephant in the room," Stuart said. "I want you to know that you won't have any issues at our end if you want to stake your claim to the throne."

"Thanks," I replied. *Stake my claim?* This felt like an episode of *Game of Thrones.*

"Unfortunately mother is insisting on a blood test before anything is definite. After all, there's no conclusive proof at the moment."

"I believe it though," Mary added quickly. "Uncle Michael always did have a reputation for... that sort of thing."

"A blood test is fine with me."

Frankly I wouldn't completely believe it myself until I saw scientific proof. It just didn't seem possible that I was related to these people. Mind you, I looked like part of the family compared to Sophia. She even ate like an American.

I smiled watching her cutting up her food into pieces before moving the fork to her right hand to eat.

"What are you laughing at?" she asked softly.

"No reason. I just think you're adorable."

"I am adorable, and don't you forget it mister."

"Impossible," I replied. "Absolutely impossible."

_*_

106

"We've prepared the largest guest room for the two of you," Jeeves said, as he showed us to our room. That had to be his name. If it wasn't, I'd make him change it when he worked for me.

"Thank you," Sophia said before darting into the room. I'd seen women in a rush to get into the bedroom before, but they were usually dragging me through with them. "Oh thank God for that," she yelled, as I closed the door.

"You didn't enjoy dinner?"

"Yeah, dinner was fine. I just need to get out of these shoes. My feet are killing me."

"Come here." I took her hand and dragged her over to the armchair in the corner. "Sit," I commanded.

She didn't so much sit as fall, but she ended up in the armchair anyway. I grabbed another chair and sat down by her legs, so that she could rest her feet on my lap.

"If you think you're going to get me into bed with a foot massage," Sophia said, as I took hold of her feet, "you have another thing coming. I'm not some innocent young... oh shit, that feels good."

She moaned sensually as I pressed my thumbs firmly into the arches of her foot and pushed up to the toes.

"Good job we have some privacy," I said, as Sophia squirmed on the chair as if my fingers were a lot higher up her leg. "So, you've just met a prince and princess. How do you feel?"

Sophia lay back on the chair with her eyes closed, still purring gently as I rubbed her feet. "Not all that different actually. I am engaged to the heir to the throne after all. These people are insignificant by comparison."

"*These people*? Oh God, I've created a monster."

"A monster with sore feet. Now do the other one please."

I took hold of Sophia's other foot and squeezed the heel with my thumbs. Would it be completely wrong to kiss her feet? And then her calves? And then work up her thighs until I could taste the sweet goodness between her legs?

"You know, I'm getting rather uncomfortable in this dress as well," Sophia said softly.

"You want to go to bed now?"

"No. I just want you to get me out of this dress."

Chapter Seventeen

SOPHIA

I should have taken a picture of this moment. George looked lost for words. How often did that happen?

He snapped out of his trance when his phone vibrated aggressively in his pocket.

"Shit." He pulled the phone out and went to throw it on the chair until he saw who the message was from.

I saw the name too; Tabitha. The woman he'd been speaking to after our wedding. The woman he loved. An undeniable feeling of jealousy washed over me every time I thought about that moment. I dealt with it by trying not to think about. Perhaps that wasn't a great long-term solution, but it would do for now.

It had almost worked. I'd barely thought about Tabatha at all tonight. Thoughts of her were buried so deep in the back of my mind, that I'd been about to give in and sleep with George. He clearly wanted to, and didn't seem to feel guilty about betraying this other woman. What did that say about him?

George typed out a quick reply, and turned his phone off. "Sorry about that. No more interruptions."

It was too late for that. The moment had passed.

"Who is she?" I asked. I knew I sounded like a crazy, jealous girlfriend, but we were married, and I'd been about to screw him. I was entitled to ask about this other woman he loved and was messaging while he was with me.

"Just someone asking me about the big dinner," George replied. "It doesn't matter. Let's pick up where we left off."

"You're in love with her."

"Huh?"

"I heard you." I hadn't been spying on him. No point pretending I hadn't heard. "You spoke to her just after we got married, and you told her you loved her."

"Oh. Well, yes, I suppose that's true."

"You 'suppose' you're in love with someone else?"

We both knew what I'd left unsaid. Why couldn't he love someone else? He wasn't in love with me, and I wasn't in love with him. We might be married, but I didn't have any claim to him.

"I'm not 'in love' with her. That just sounds weird."

"What do you mean... oh," I trailed off, as I realized who the woman must have been. If the thought of being in love with someone was 'weird,' then it likely meant said person was either a very close friend, or a family member. "Cousin?" I asked.

"Close. Sister."

"You have a sister?"

"Yep."

"And don't you think you should have mentioned that before now?" I asked.

"We've never really discussed family. It's not like I know a lot about yours."

"Yes, but my family tree doesn't include a claim to the throne of the United Kingdom."

"It does now. Anyway, Tabitha doesn't have a claim. She was born a few years after my Mom's marriage to the King ended, and she has a different father. She also lives in the States, actually."

We hadn't spoken much about family because I cried every time I tried to talk about my mother. I didn't have any other family to speak of, but it had never bothered me before. My friends had all been more important to me. Then they'd betrayed me.

"Are you close?" I asked.

"Yes," George replied. "Very. In fact…"

"In fact?"

"I should have told you all this sooner."

"This isn't filling me with confidence, George."

"I know. I'm sorry." George took a deep breath and sat back down on the chair. I didn't speak; he suddenly looked like he carried the weight of the world on his shoulders. His usually strong frame, now slumped down as if he'd given up the fight. "I lied to you."

My heart skipped a beat, and then made up for the loss by pounding away in my chest at twice the speed. Now it was my turn to sit back down; better that than faint.

"What did you lie about?"

"The reason I'm doing all this," came the reply. "The reason I asked you to marry me, and the reason I want to claim my inheritance."

George reached out and placed his hand on mine, but I pushed his away and pulled mine out of reach. Our marriage hadn't exactly been under the most romantic of circumstances, but that made the lie hurt even more. I'd told him the truth about needing a visa. What could be worse than wanting to marry me just to claim a load of money and live like a playboy?

I might not want the answer to that question; I asked anyway.

"Tell me," I insisted. "We need to be completely honest with each other. I'm pretty sure that was in the vows."

"My sister, she's… not well. Neither is my nephew, her son."

"What's wrong with them?"

I sounded cold and callous grilling him on the topic of his sick family members. Maybe I was like my mother after all?

"They were in an accident a few years ago. Actually, you know what, fuck that, it wasn't an accident. They were hit by a car. A car driven at them deliberately by her ex-boyfriend. It's fucked up."

"Oh my God." I quickly reached out and placed my hand on his just like George had tried to do to me earlier. "I'm so sorry."

"They're okay," George said, squeezing my hand. "Well, they're not completely okay, obviously, but they're not on death's door or anything either."

"You need the money to look after them?" I asked.

"Yeah. They're both undergoing physical therapy, and as you may know, your country doesn't believe in providing medical care without it being accompanied by a fucking huge invoice."

"I had noticed. I'm almost tempted to have an accident while I'm here just to make use of the NHS."

George smiled and squeezed my hand more tightly. "I should have told you."

"Yes, you should have. I've been imagining you living like a player on your new fortune. I feel bad for your sister and nephew, but I'd rather the money go to them than bottles of champagne and loose women."

George laughed out loud and pulled me up out of my seat and flying onto his lap. "I don't actually like champagne, and I'm hoping to just live it up with one loose woman for the time being."

"I am not loose," I insisted.

"You're assuming I'm talking about you."

"You'd better be," I replied.

George laughed again, but this time the laugh stopped quickly. He reached up and held the back of my neck, before bringing me down towards him for a kiss.

Chapter Eighteen

SOPHIA

I kissed him back passionately. I think that took him by surprise almost as much as it did me. We both expected me to put up a fight, or make things awkward, but I couldn't. The incessant throbbing between my legs had become too much to resist; if I didn't act on it now, I'd end up going insane.

Our bodies melted together as our tongues clashed in my mouth and George's cock pressed up against my waist. His scent filled my nose, while his touch awoke my body. I was totally, utterly, and completely lost in the moment. We were in a royal residence, but we could have been anywhere right now. I wouldn't have cared if we were in a bus shelter with an audience. Nothing could have spoiled this moment.

George guided me towards the bed, and then pushed me away from him the second the foot of the bed brushed against my knees. I fell backwards, but immediately propped myself back up onto my elbows to check out the view.

For a few moments, George just stood there looking down at me from the foot of the bed, as if he might change his mind at any moment. Then he reached up to the top of his shirt and slowly started undoing the buttons.

I'd never seen his chest. It sounded ridiculous, but I'd never seen my husband's chest. There was plenty of him I'd never seen, but his chest was all I could focus on right now.

His shirt opened and fell to the floor. I heard the sound of his belt buckle opening, but I didn't look down; I couldn't take my eyes off his chest. I could swear it was staring back at me. The firm pecs—tattoos encroaching on them from his shoulders—seemed to be eying me up, challenging me to look away. I couldn't do it. I had to take it all in, committing it to memory as if I would later have to draw it for a police sketch. He had more contours and ridges than a fingerprint, and I was willing to bet good money that this body was one-hundred-percent unique.

I hadn't even noticed how wet I was getting between my burning thighs, but when George dropped his pants—taking his boxers with them—I finally had a reason to look away from his chest.

"Damn," I muttered, as I watched his cock quickly grow hard in front of me.

"That's a common reaction," he replied with a grin.

I sat up and wrapped my hands around the shaft, stroking slowly, as if experimenting with something new and foreign. Size-wise, it most definitely was new. I'd seen my share of cocks, but this one was something else. It throbbed in my palm, as I moved my hand up to the head and squeezed gently, eking out a bit of cum from the tip.

There was no way a girl could resist that.

I moved my head towards his shaft and opened wide to take him into my hot, wet mouth. I breathed deeply through my nose, before sliding my lips down the smooth skin of his cock. His member pulsed in my mouth, ready to explode.

"Sophia," George moaned deeply, as my lips got as far down his shaft as they were going to. I'd always been proud of my gag reflex—or lack of it—but there was only so much room in my mouth and throat.

He clasped my head with both of his hands and held it in position with my lips most of the way down his cock. I concentrated on breathing through my nose, while he slowly pushed his cock deeper down my throat. I expected him to empty himself inside me at any second, but instead he pulled all the way out, leaving a trail of saliva from my lips to the tip of his cock.

"It's impossible to control myself around you," George said through deep breaths. He unzipped the back of my dress, and then moved up on the bed, dragging me up with him until my head was resting on the pillow.

I closed my eyes and tried to calm my nerves as George pulled my dress off and threw it to the floor. I couldn't see anything, but I could feel his eyes on me as I lay there in just my bra and panties. His body was so perfect, sculpted, literally like a work of art. Mine was… normal. I was young enough that my breasts still pointed up, and I was slim, but I didn't have a lot else going for me. There were freckles, and soft bits that wouldn't disappear no matter how many sit ups I did in front of the television.

"You're stunning," George said softly.

I opened my eyes and looked up at him. He was staring down at me with a genuine look of desire on his face. I wasn't stunning, but George seemed to think so, and that was just fine with me.

He leaned down and kissed me on the lips, his hard cock pressing eagerly against my belly. A hand went under my back and unclasped my bra, quickly whipping it off in one smooth motion.

The second my breasts were free, his mouth dived onto a nipple, covering it with his warm lips, and flicking against it with his tongue. This time it was my turn to hold his head and keep him close to me.

"Oh, George," I moaned as he bit down gently on my erect nipple. His hand slid down my stomach towards my panties which were getting wetter and wetter with every second my nipple was in his mouth.

His fingers pressed against my sex from the outside of the soaking wet cotton between my legs. I tried to pull his head up to mine—desperate to get his body on top of me—but he resisted and instead headed in the other direction.

His lips kissed my skin as his mouth made its way slowly down to my underwear. Each kiss sent jolts through my body, and left behind a fire on my skin, until finally George crawled between my legs, and hooked his fingers under my panties.

They came off in a blur, and suddenly my wet sex was exposed to George. He looked down between my legs with hunger filling his eyes. I needed him to devour me and I couldn't wait any longer. I hooked my legs around him and pulled his body down between his legs.

"You're not the patient type, are you?" he asked.

"Are you?"

"Good point."

George's mouth kissed the insides of my quivering thighs as he slowly made his way down to my wet slit. The second his tongue touched my sex, the built-up anticipation washed over me and left me gasping for breath on the bed.

I looked down between my legs; our eyes met briefly before George sent his tongue darting out to my swollen clit.

My head snapped back and my eyes closed shut as George ate me with a furious intensity. My hands gripped the covers, but nothing I did could keep the pleasure at bay. My hips rocked furiously against his mouth as he slipped his tongue into my entrance, groaning with pleasure as he ate me.

"You taste so fucking gorgeous," he murmured, his tongue coming out and sliding back up to my clit.

I cried out in pleasure, although I don't think any of the sounds formed actual words. They were just noises that had to come out.

I kept squirming under the expert touch of his tongue, but his hands clasped my hips firmly, so that his tongue never left my wetness. Every movement of his tongue sent shock waves throughout my body until I was finally ready to let go and surrender.

Then he stopped.

His mouth left my sex, and suddenly my world felt empty.

"Bad timing," I gasped, as I lay shaking on the bed. I'd been right on the edge and but didn't go over.

"Perfect timing," he replied from the side of the bed. He must have dug a condom out of his pocket, because he came back to the bed with his cock sheathed and ready to go. "I want to feel you come around my cock."

George climbed on top and kissed me deeply, letting me taste the sweetness that covered his mouth and chin. His cock moved close to my entrance, but he let it stay there just out of reach as we embraced and kissed.

I'd been excited by the size of his manhood, but now I realized that somehow he was going to have to squeeze that thing inside me. The prospect had me equal parts nervous and excited, but the increasing wetness between my thighs made it clear that my excitement would win the battle in my mind.

I wrapped my legs around George and slowly pushed him into me, encouraging him to enter and finish what he'd started. He guided his huge length to my opening and then pushed forward slowly as he filled me inch by glorious, pulsating inch.

He looked into my eyes as he rocked his hips on top of me. The gasps of discomfort at his size quickly turned into whimpers of joy, as my sex flooded with pleasure at every movement of his cock inside me.

George was holding back. I wanted him to let go and lose himself in my sex, but I was in no position to give any commands. All I could do was lay there, squirming and moaning, as his cock warmed my insides and spread fire throughout my body.

"Keep going," I murmured.

"You're so tight," he moaned, as his cock slid deep into me. "I don't know how long I can last."

The muscles in my sex clenched hold of his pulsating cock, as if it never wanted to let go. I leaned back into the pillow and cried out, losing myself completely in the moment, as his cock finally sent me over the edge that I'd been teetering on since he kissed me. Hell, I'd been waiting for this since we first met.

George shook and groaned deeply, as his cock throbbed and then emptied inside me. We kissed again, before he rolled to one side and we lay next to each other, breathless, on the large four-poster bed.

As first times with a new guy went, doing it in a royal residence was right up there. It certainly beat my first time with Stan in more ways than one.

The sound of creaking floorboards came from outside the room as servants shuffled around tidying up and getting the house prepared for the morning.

"Do you think they heard us?" I asked George nervously.

"I don't think so. But they might hear the next time."

"Next t—" My words got lost in my throat as George pressed his lips up against mine and brought me in towards him. His cock wasn't just huge—it was insatiable.

Chapter Nineteen

GEORGE

Neither of us could go home. My apartment building was continually surrounded by reporters, cameras, and television crews, while Sophia's had become almost like a shrine for young girls in the area who wanted to see where the princess had been living when she met her prince.

We booked a long term stay in a London hotel under assumed names, and acquired entirely new wardrobes to save the hassle of moving. Ellie and Dani had come in use again on that front, by bringing some of the essentials from our apartments to the hotel.

"Was this how you envisioned your honeymoon?" I asked my wife, as she lay on the bed knocking back chocolates that had been one of the many gifts we'd had shoved into our hands over the past few days.

"Stan and I were supposed to spend two weeks in Barbados, soaking up the sun on the beach and swimming in the clear blue seas."

"So that's a 'no' then?"

"I burn easily, and I hate beaches. The sand gets everywhere. I'm also an awful swimmer. I'm happy here with you."

"What type of grand holiday would you like to go on? Walking the Great Wall of China? Hiking? Skiing?"

"I've always wanted to ski. I grew up just a few hours from Lake Tahoe, but we couldn't afford the lessons and all the gear you needed. Can you ski?"

"I'm English. The only thing I can do on snow is fall on my arse. We did have a dry ski slope near where I lived, but I never went."

"Dry ski slope? That sounds painful."

"It probably is. True story—there was one time me and some friends were going to go there for a birthday party. We were all excited, and a little nervous, but it had been snowing recently, so we were all in the skiing mood."

"I thought you said you'd never been."

"I haven't. The dry ski slope had to shut because of the snow. That's skiing in Britain for you."

"Sounds like we both want to ski."

"I'll take you," I promised. "Once all this is over, I'll pay for a skiing holiday. Or I'll pay for you to go with your friends if you'd prefer."

"No, we can go together. It'll be fun. A celebration of tricking everyone with a fake marriage."

The marriage didn't feel all that fake at the moment. We were living under the same roof, sleeping together, and planning holidays. If we started arguing over the chores and stopped having sex, then it would be a completely bona fide marriage.

"How long until room service arrives?" Sophia asked. "I'm starving."

"About twenty minutes," I replied. "That's just about time for—"

"Uh-uh. I don't have the energy for that. Food first, then sex."

"It's good to work up an appetite."

"We worked up an appetite an hour ago. We're just still waiting for the food to arrive."

"You know, it's not often women turn me down."

"Better get used to it, buster; we're married now."

"I could have you right now if I wanted you," I said with a smile.

Sophia legs fidgeted under the covers, giving me all the confirmation I needed. *This hotel had better hurry up with the food.*

"Stop being a cocky git and pass me the remote."

"A cocky git?" I asked.

"Yeah. That's what you people say isn't it?"

"I have never been more proud of you." I threw Sophia the remote and just prayed that she wasn't into reality television. How crazy was that? I didn't even know what types of television shows my wife watched.

Sophia flicked through the channels aimlessly, barely stopping on each one for a second before moving onto the next.

"How can you even tell what the show is?" I asked.

"I can tell," she replied. "Ah, here we go. Let's watch the fight."

"What fight?"

"It's the big UFC championship match. How have you not heard of it; It's been hyped for weeks. US versus the UK. England versus America. Batman versus… no, wait, that's something different."

"You like this rubbish?" I asked.

I liked boxing, and I'd always thought of UFC as being a less disciplined, more bloodthirsty version of that. The UFC crowds bayed for blood in much the same way as an audience at a wrestling match. It didn't really do anything for me.

"Ellie, Dani, and I always watch it when we can. It's quite entertaining after a few bottles of wine."

I glanced up at the television as the British fighter—Elliot Michaels—was introduced to the home crowd.

"I think I've just figured out why you like watching this," I said, as I watched Elliot stroll up towards the cage.

"Touch jealous, are we?" Sophia teased.

"Not likely. I have all the muscles they do, and my tattoos are better."

"You sound jealous."

"Actually, I am," I admitted. Elliot's team gathered around him before the fight, which included a young woman holding a medical bag. "My doctor is nowhere near that attractive."

"Yeah, well, unfortunately for you, she isn't about to get half-naked and work up a sweat on television. This will be my little treat before dinner."

A phone call from Harry gave me a decent excuse not to watch this crap.

"What's up Harry?"

"I've got good news—the public is loving that little walking tour you did of London earlier. I'll give you your dues, that was a damn good play. Visiting all those independent shops makes you look like a real 'community values' kind of guy."

"Thanks."

I hated it when Harry made this all sound so artificial. I knew it was, but I didn't like hearing it from others. Sophia and I could talk that way about it, but no one else.

"The palace visit also went down well. You're coming across as mature and sensible, which is quite remarkable for you."

"Thanks again, Harry."

"You're welcome. Anyway, I want you to do another event in the public eye. Something to really make you look like a prince and heir to the throne."

"I don't want to look like a prince," I insisted. "We need to look like a couple, but I'm never going to become a prince, and I'm sure as hell never going to be king."

I'd let Harry in on the secret, because he started getting his hopes up about being a full-time PR person for the royal family. I'd done my best to let him down gently, but he hadn't taken the news well.

"I was hoping you'd changed your mind about that."

"Nope. This is not about me becoming a prince. It's about me getting the inheritance I'm entitled to."

"Alright, alright, you win. But you should do another appearance anyway. One more won't hurt."

Harry was right. We needed to look like a couple or the trustees wouldn't be convinced by the marriage. We could buy a house, or make some other grand commitment, but a few public appearances were a lot easier and quicker. The sooner I got the money, the sooner we could go back to our normal lives.

That would be a mixed blessing. I'd have money, but I wouldn't have Sophia. There was always the skiing holiday to look forward to, though. If that's how things had to end between us, then it would be a fun way to go out.

"Okay, one more event," I agreed. "But nothing with the royal family. That would send a mixed message."

"Deal."

"Thanks Harry."

I hung up and looked back at Sophia. I'd been hoping she was too transfixed by the fight to have paid attention to my conversation, but she'd clearly picked up the gist of it.

"What are we doing next?" she asked.

"I don't know yet. Nothing major."

"Okay, well that's fine with me. We might need pictures of us together when applying for my visa. Helps to prove the relationship is real."

"You know, if you wanted to prove we have a genuine relationship, then we could take some photos that would be conclusive proof—"

"No," Sophia snapped immediately. "Not happening, mister."

"Shame. You look so damn good when you're down on your knees sucking my—"

"Room service," came a call from the door.

I grabbed our food and presented Sophia with her tray since she didn't look like she had any intention on getting out of bed.

"I should have ordered more," she said. "I'm famished."

"You have a burger, fries, Oreo cookie milkshake, and a chocolate tart for dessert. Surely you can't eat all that?"

"I'm always hungry after sex," she replied, shoving fries into her mouth.

"Guess I'd better start leaving snacks by the bed."

"It'd be wise." She paused to eat, and then stopped to drink some of her milkshake. "You haven't changed your mind about becoming a prince?"

"Nope. Not at all. Why'd you ask?"

I knew the answer. She wanted to be a princess, and god damn it, she deserved to be one. I wished I could give her that, but I couldn't. That's not what this was about.

"You just shouldn't be so quick to write it off. You could do a lot of good as a prince, and you'd still have loads of money."

"But I need the money for Tabitha; you know that."

"Yes, but I've heard rumors that princes are actually quite well off."

"I won't be able to spend taxpayer funds on my sister."

"As long as you're sure."

"I'm sure," I insisted, as Sophia went back to eating.

I watched as she took a large bite from the burger and piled a few more fries into her mouth. I had to shove food into my own mouth just to stop myself from laughing. I had no idea how anyone so petite could eat so much and not put on weight. Even stranger, I found the sight of her eating one of the sexiest things I'd ever seen. There was nothing this girl could possibly do to put me off.

Then Sophia belched.

She quickly covered her mouth with her hand and gasped, but didn't look round at me. I bit my lip hard, but in the end the laugh slipped out anyway. Once I laughed Sophia went bright red and tried to hide her face in her hands.

I wrapped my arm around her shoulder and brought her gently towards me, being careful not to knock any of the trays over.

"You're absolutely adorable, you know that?"

Chapter Twenty

SOPHIA

One day soon, we'd have to leave this place, and I'd have to go back to college, but for now I didn't intend to move an inch more than I had to.

I woke up to a message on my phone from George. *Be back soon. Need to see a man about a dog. Keep the bed warm for me.*

I'll be in the shower when you get back. Come in and join me.

We'd been screwing all day, and the day before that, so I seemed to be constantly sweaty and sticky no matter how many times we shared a shower. Actually, sharing a shower often led to us getting sweaty and sticky again.

My phone vibrated on the marble surface next to the sink and then fell to the floor before I could grab it. I should have known George would reply to that message. Probably something filthy.

There was no text message, but an email had come through. I'd turned all email notifications off after George and I went public, but I'd forgotten about an old Gmail account that I didn't use any more.

I'd switched to a new account after splitting with Stan, and everyone had my new email address. Everyone except Stan.

Hi gorgeous,

Long time no see.

Blood drained from my face, and I felt dizzy and sick at the same time. The urge to vomit kept me in the bathroom, but I sat down on the cold marble floor before I fainted.

Seems you've come into money. Or rather your new husband has.

I guess this is where I say congratulations. Congratulations! I'm happy for you, I really am. And I'm happy for myself too. I didn't think you'd ever be able to repay me for the pain, and emotional distress I went through after you ran out on our wedding, but now it looks like you can.

That wedding wasn't cheap, plus you embarrassed me in front of my friends and family. $1,000,000 should cover it.

Don't even think about showing this to the police or pretending you can't afford it. I want the money and if you can't give it to me, I'll just have to find some other way to profit from this mess.

Hmm… whatever could I sell to make some money…

I frowned at the cryptic ending to the email, and read it again. What would he sell? Stories about us? I suppose he could say I was shit in bed, but there would likely be men coming out and saying the opposite. If they didn't, I might give them a nudge. The public deserved to hear both sides of every story after all.

It wasn't until I closed the email that I spotted the paperclip next to it, showing that there was an attachment. Not just one attachment—twenty-two. Photos, short video clips, and a few screenshots of text messages.

The messages were from me and they were graphic. Nowhere near as graphic as the photos and video clips though. Some of them were just body shots, but there were plenty containing my face in varying stages of excitement. One picture even showed my face with evidence of Stan's excitement all over it. The videos were all of me touching myself waiting for Stan to join me at home. I'd been bored and—much to my continued amazement—I used to desire him.

Now the entire country was about to see its princess—and possible future queen—in a way that only her boyfriend of the time was ever supposed to see.

I closed my eyes and prayed for the floor to open up and swallow me. I couldn't handle this. There was a reason Princes and Princesses were kept in a bubble from birth. It was so they didn't do anything foolish like sending nude photos to their partners or making homemade sex tapes.

There had to be a way out of this. If George never officially accepted his role as a prince, then as far as Stan knew, he wouldn't have any money. We didn't have to make the inheritance public knowledge. Stan might still release the photos out of spite, but he wouldn't be able to blackmail me.

George didn't want to be a prince anyway, and I sure as hell didn't want to become a princess if it meant that videos of me touching myself, slick and wet with excitement, ended up all over the Internet. I'd go down in history with one of those awful nicknames like Slutty Sophia, or The Randy Princess.

"Everything okay?" George asked.

I opened my eyes and looked up from my position still sat on the cold bathroom floor. I hadn't even noticed him come in. How long had I been here for? I still felt sick to my stomach. Stan could release those photos and videos at any minute. How long would it take that information to get out online? Three, maybe four seconds?

"Yeah," I said, pushing myself up to my feet. "I'm fine. Just figured I'd wait for you before getting in the shower. Is that man's dog okay?"

George frowned, but then laughed. "I wasn't actually seeing... Nevermind. God, you're adorable. Come here."

George wrapped his arms around me and hugged me tightly. His hands were freezing cold on my back, but I didn't flinch away.

I should tell him. If he changed his mind and decided to become a prince, this would be as much an issue for him as it would for me. Not to mention, it would be a national embarrassment.

I felt dirty, and not in a good way. What had I been thinking? I'd been in love with Stan at the time, but I should have known better than to do something so permanent.

"So, uh, why were you sat on the bathroom floor?" George asked.

"Just thinking."

"About?"

"About whether I want to be a princess after all. I'm coming around to your way of thinking. Perhaps it's just best if claim the inheritance, and then... you know."

"Go our separate ways?

"Yeah. After spending an appropriate amount of time together of course."

"Of course," George agreed. "Wouldn't want to risk it looking fake. Maybe we should be together a little longer than we initially planned?"

"Fine with me."

"Still want a shower?" George asked.

"Why don't we see if this bath is big enough for two?"

"Sounds perfect."

Chapter Twenty-One

GEORGE

"I feel like a right tit."

"Well I think you look absolutely adorable," Sophia said, as she looked me up and down.

"You're not allowed to call me that," I insisted. "That's my word for you."

"Okay, then you look handsome," Sophia said.

"I'd be a lot more convinced if you weren't covering your mouth with your hand to stifle a laugh."

I never in a million years thought I would be seen dead with tight white trousers, knee high leather boots, and a whip.

"You two ready?" Harry asked, before looking me up and down. "Um, George, you don't need a whip for polo."

"*Someone* told me I did," I said tersely, staring at Sophia, who was still trying not to laugh.

"You just need this stick," Harry said, taking the whip from me and passing Sophia and me long sticks with a club at the end. "Simple game really. You just need to use this to hit the ball in the goal."

"Simple," Sophia said.

"Yeah," I agreed, "except we'll be doing it on horses."

"You'll be fine," Sophia said. "It's easy. Like riding a bike. Kind of."

"You've ridden before?" Harry asked.

"Yeah, she's used to riding a horse," I joked.

"A few times," Sophia replied, after elbowing me in the ribs. "A friend from school used to own a horse, and she let me ride it occasionally."

"But you haven't, George?"

"No," I replied. "We weren't really the horse riding type growing up."

"You'll get the hang of it soon enough."

I didn't.

_*_

"Remind me why we're doing this again?" I yelled to Sophia as she rode past me chasing after the ball. I tried to turn the horse around, but by the time I had done so, the ball was heading back in the other direction. I should just play goalkeeper. Did they have goalkeepers in this sport?

"It's for charity," she yelled back.

So this is what the nobility did in its spare time—faffed around on horses for other rich people to watch. My schoolmates were going to have a great fucking laugh when these pictures came out.

I had no hope of making any contribution to the team, so I just watched Sophia riding gracefully around the field as if she'd been doing this sort of thing her entire life. She dangled so far over the side of the horse in an effort to reach the ball, it was a miracle she didn't fall off. I, on the other hand, could barely stay on the horse even though I was making no effort to play the ball.

As usual, Sophia looked perfect. I never could keep my eyes off her when she wore tight trousers, and right now the trousers were so tight I could see her thighs tensing as she fought to stay in control of the horse between her legs.

Men like me were not meant to ride horses. I was way too fucking big for one thing. I should be playing rugby, or, at a push, football. I'd rather play cricket than this shit, and that was really saying something given my general hatred for that 'sport.'

People on my team started shouting my name while horses from the opposing team sped towards me. I looked down and saw the ball lying still next to my horse. I should probably do something.

I leant over and swung the big club-thing in my hand. I made contact with the ball and sent it somewhere in Sophia's general direction. Then the momentum of my swing brought my club all the way round, and made me lose balance.

Turns out losing balance while riding a horse— badly—is not a good combination. I fell. Frankly, I was amazed it took so long. I hadn't been particularly high up, but I still managed to hit the ground with an almighty thud.

I froze and stayed still as hooves thundered past me, barely avoiding trampling all over me.

I bloody hated horses.

_*_

"We've raised a record amount for charity," Harry said excitedly as he slapped me on my bruised back. "Your appearance here really made a difference. Falling off the horse probably helped as well."

"Glad I did some good," I replied.

Next time I'm staying in the bedroom with Sophia. I've never fallen off a bed before.

"Look," Harry continued, "usually all this money would go to the Prince's Trust, which I guess you may take over soon, but I've convinced the organizers to let you nominate the charity."

"Oh sure," I replied. "Let's give it to the Mary Kay Foundation."

An easy choice for me, given what had happened to my sister, although a few hundred pounds wasn't going to go too far in the grand scheme of themes. Still every little bit helped.

"Excellent, I'll get it set up."

I looked around for Sophia and saw her running over to me from the stables where she'd spent some time with the horses.

"You'll be pleased to know your horse didn't suffer any injuries," Sophia said, as she stretched up and kissed me on the cheek.

"Oh, excellent," I replied sarcastically. "I'm delighted to hear that. I was so worried about the creature. As I was falling, all I could think was 'I hope the horse is okay.'"

"If you'd have listened to the training, you would have had your feet in the stirrups properly and you wouldn't have fallen off."

"I was too distracted by you in those tight trousers."

I reached around and squeezed her arse firmly before she slapped my hand away.

"There are cameras everywhere." She flushed red and bit her lower lip, which meant we would be heading back to the hotel as soon as possible.

"Let's get out of here," I whispered in her ear.

"Okay, but I am not straddling anything tonight. My thighs are killing me."

We were just about to sneak away when I heard Harry's voice over the loudspeakers dotted around the field.

"Thank you ladies and gentlemen for coming here today. And thank you for bringing your cheque books." A gentle laughter rippled over the crowd which by this point was giddy with champagne. "As you all know, we had a special guest here today." The crowd all turned to face me which meant I had to force a smile and wave. "Mr.

Whittemore has nominated the chosen charity, so we will be sending a check for £135,000 to The Mary Kay Foundation."

There was probably more applause at this point, but I was too stunned to notice.

"Was I hearing things," I asked Sophia, "or did he just say £135,000?"

"It's a wealthy crowd."

"Holy. Shit."

Maybe being a prince isn't that bad after all.

The second Harry had finished his little speech, I escaped the crowds and got changed into some normal-people clothes.

"Ready to head back to the hotel?" Sophia asked. Then she leaned close and whispered in my ear. "I've kept the boots."

I groaned in anticipation, and was about ready to pick her up in my arms and carry her back to the waiting limo when I remembered something else we should be taking back with us.

Harry ran over the second I caught his eye.

"What's up, George?"

"Uh, I'm going to need that whip back."

Chapter Twenty-Two

GEORGE

There was nothing more wonderful in life than a woman who had no idea just how beautiful she was.

She kept catching me staring at her in the car on the way to the hotel. I probably looked like a creepy stalker, but I just couldn't take my eyes off her. Here was a woman who could get me going just by sitting cross-legged in the car and typing out text messages on her phone.

Sophia wasn't perfect. Even though she was no shrinking violet—not by any stretch of the imagination—she hadn't let me bring the whip back to the hotel room. Something about not wanting to be treated like a horse. There was just no pleasing some women.

The second I had money, I'd insist on a limo to drive us around everywhere. At least that way we would have privacy. I couldn't bear sitting in the car for twenty minutes without being able to rip the clothes from her body and devour every inch of her.

But of course, the second I had money, we would split up and go our separate ways. That was the plan after all.

I forced those thoughts from my mind when the car pulled up next to the hotel, and the driver opened the door. We would soon have some privacy; that was all that mattered right now.

My balls were heavy and my cock throbbed in my pants. I'd once gone a week without release when I was a teenager as part of a dare. That's what this felt like, except one hundred times worse because Sophia was right beside me, her presence a constant tease on my already-strained patience.

The ache—bordering on pain—got worse with every second I wasn't inside her tight, wet sex. Did she feel the same way? She looked to be handling the wait with remarkable ease, whereas I was about to explode.

We didn't speak as the elevator moved painfully slowly up to the top floor. I dug the keycard from my wallet—eventually finding it hidden between loads of credit cards—and we stumbled into the room. We'd been alone in the elevator, but even so, the door slamming shut signaled an end to being under public scrutiny for the time being.

That meant sex.

At fucking last.

"You look tense," Sophia teased.

"You have no bloody idea," I replied.

"Want me to order a massage? They have a nice young man called Diego on staff. He'll come up to the room if you want."

"The only hands I want on my skin are yours. Come here."

Sophia bit her lip, and for a painful moment I thought she might play hard to get. She turned her back and walked slowly towards the bed. Standing with her back to me, she pulled off her top, before dropping it on the floor.

"Stay there," she commanded, just as I went to half walk, half fly across the room towards her.

Sophia reached a hand behind her and unclasped her bra, letting it fall softly to the floor. It took all my willpower not to dive over there. Just knowing her breasts were exposed had my cock straining to be set free. Her nipples would be stiff, eagerly awaiting my warm mouth.

Next came her trousers. Sophia hooked her thumbs under the waistband and—excruciatingly slowly—pulled them down to her knees, before bending at the waist and taking them all the way down to the floor. At some point, she stepped out of them, but my eyes were too transfixed on her arse—barely covered by her skimpy knickers—as she pointed it at me, challenging me to move from my spot.

Finally, Sophia turned around to face me, wearing just her panties. "You like?" she asked.

"I'd like them a lot more on the floor."

Sophia smiled, and slipped her panties off just as she had done her trousers before.

I didn't know where to look.

"You can come over now," she said.

How long had I been standing there for? I was almost drooling at this point.

I resisted the urge to run up and throw her down on the bed. Instead, I walked up, and kissed her softly on the lips, as if were a mature adult in a relationship. Weird.

Sophia moaned in my mouth as our tongues met. My hands began exploring the soft skin of her back while she wrapped her arms around my neck and held on tight.

I couldn't kiss her for long before the urge to take her breasts in my mouth became impossible to resist. Sophia sighed as I circled a nipple with my tongue, while pinching the other gently between thumb and forefinger so it didn't feel left out.

"You need to get naked," Sophia said between heavy breaths.

"Yes, m'lady." I'd never undressed so quickly. The second I was naked, Sophia was handing me something else to wear. I tore open the packet with my teeth and quickly sheathed myself.

This time I did push her to the bed. She fell down with her legs invitingly open, but instead of diving between them, I lay down next to her and continued caressing her skin.

Sophia held her breath as my fingers trickled over her breasts, down to her belly, and then to her sex. My fingers brushed lightly against her soaking folds, but I didn't enter her. She was ready for me, and I wanted my cock to be what took her from the starting line all the way to the finish.

"You're so beautiful," I muttered, as I moved my hand to her thigh.

"Fit for a prince?" she joked.

"Fit for a king."

"I'll settle for a prince for now."

My hand moved back up to her chest, where I felt her heart pounding against my palm. "You nervous?"

"No. Excited."

I leaned over her and pressed my lips against hers as I moved between her legs and guided my cock to her slick entrance. I looked into her eyes as I plunged myself deep inside her. Sophia moaned deeply, and wrapped her arms around my back as I filled her completely.

Her hips rocked in time with mine, as my cock slipped in and out of her increasing wetness. I knew that her breasts would be pert and her nipples hard, but I couldn't take break my gaze from her eyes.

Time lost all meaning. We were in rhythm with each other, body and mind, and I lost myself completely in the moment. It could have been a minute later or twenty minutes later, but at some point, I felt the muscles in her body tensing up. Her fingers dug tighter into my back, and her pussy clenched hold of my cock, reluctant to let me leave her.

She came in almost complete silence. Only the tension of her body and then the eventual release let me know that she had finished.

"Come on me," Sophia whispered in my ear. "I want to feel your excitement on my skin."

Those perky breasts were crying out to be covered in cum; it was a miracle they'd stayed dry this long. I thrust harder and faster, bringing myself right to the edge, like I had done with Sophia.

Just in time, I pulled out, rolled off the thin silicone covering my pulsating shaft, and then shot my load all over her perfect breasts. Shot after shot splattered onto her chest and belly, until I was completely spent.

I collapsed back down next to Sophia and admired the Jackson Pollock painting I'd made of her body.

"This is where you get me a towel," Sophia said, as she lay there rigid, unable to move without my release dripping down her.

"Nah, I think I'll just leave you like this."

"If you do, I'm going to lean over and give you a nice, sticky cuddle."

"I'll get a towel."

Sophia wiped herself clean and then we did cuddle; it was still a little sticky, but I'd never push her away. I wanted to hold her in my arms and never let go.

But we were on a timer. At some point, we would go our separate ways again.

Sophia squeezed me tightly as if she were thinking the exact same thing. Maybe she was.

I returned the squeeze and kissed her firmly on the forehead, as she rested on my chest. Somehow she fell asleep, despite my heart pounding heavily against her ear.

I stayed awake as long as possible, just watching her breathing, but eventually I closed my eyes and drifted off for a much needed post-sex nap. This time there was no need to slip out from under her and do a runner. I was right where I wanted to be.

Chapter Twenty-Three

SOPHIA

I didn't mean to touch it.

Even after napping yesterday afternoon, I'd still fallen asleep within minutes of closing my eyes when we'd finally stopped screwing and gone to sleep. During the night, I must have turned over and rolled away from George, so the first thing I did on waking up was turn over and rest my head on his chest.

My hand went to his stomach, and there *it* was. Hard, and ready to go.

"Morning, gorgeous," George said, sounding like he'd had twice as much sleep as me. I could barely open my mouth to speak, and, given my morning breath, that was probably for the best.

Was it possible to hear a twinkle in someone's eye? I didn't have to look up to him to picture the look on his face. The throbbing hard cock under the palm of my hand did kind of give it away.

"How do you have any life left in this thing?" I asked, giving his cock a casual shake. "I'm surprised it hasn't fallen off after last night."

"It's like a muscle—the more you train it, the stronger it becomes."

I tried not to think too hard about all the "coaches" who'd helped train George's manhood over the years. I didn't care—not really—but it wasn't exactly an image I wanted to keep in my mind. I'd had my share of coaches after all. Not as many as George, but a decent enough number that I was no longer playing in the minor leagues.

"Got any energy for a training session this morning?" I asked. I wrapped my fingers around his cock and stroked it slowly. Every pulse of the vein against my palm had me wetter and wetter between the legs, as I anticipated feeling it inside me.

"No training," George replied. "I've been training for the last ten years. You're the main event. You're what I've been training for."

I propped myself up on one elbow and looked at George while I kept stroking his shaft. "You're saying you slept with all those other women for my benefit?"

"Anything for you, sweetheart."

I laughed and shook my head. "You're really lucky that I want this cock in me, or we would be having a very different discussion."

I quickly rolled away and looked down at the floor, littered with clothes, condom wrappers, and—fortunately—one last condom still in its wrapper. George held out his hand for the condom, but I pushed it to one side and tore open the packet myself. If men could manage it, how hard could it be?

I pinched the tip of the condom and slowly rolled it all the way down to the base. Even sheathed, I could still feel it throbbing away in my hand, like it might explode at any second.

George pulled me towards him, and kissed me deeply. If he cared about my morning breath, he didn't show it. His hands squeezed my breasts firmly while I reached a hand down between his legs and guided his cock into my sex.

Slowly, I pushed my hips down and took him inside me, my wetness immediately soaking the condom and the hair around the base of his cock.

God, I needed that, I thought as I rocked gently on top of him. Had it really only been a few hours? My hands rested on George's chest, my nails digging into the skin wrapped tightly around his muscular torso, while I rode myself to the edge and then quickly over it.

Practice really did make perfect.

_*_

When I was in George's arms I felt safe, secure, and happy. When he let go, I couldn't think of anything other than the email from Stan. I stared at my computer, knowing that if I opened it up and logged into my email, I would find the blackmail attempt and the ammunition to back it up.

Stan could destroy my life with the press of a button, but I could still cling to the hope that he wouldn't do it once George renounced the throne. Stan was a bastard, but he'd never been vindictive. If he'd wanted to punish me for leaving him at the altar, he could have released the photos a year ago. He probably thought I still had some of him, but I'd gotten a new laptop and phone when I moved to the UK, and I'd never uploaded our sex photos to the cloud. Still, it would be a good idea to let Stan think I had some of him as well. It's not like they would get much public attention, but they would still embarrass him. He hadn't exactly been as naturally 'gifted' as George in the downstairs department.

George strolled back into the bedroom wearing just his boxers, and climbed back into bed next to me. "They want me to do another charity event. The last one raised a record amount of money."

"People really are suckers for a pretty face," I replied.

"It's got nothing to do with me. Everyone loves us as a couple. You make a beautiful princess."

A few days ago, those words would have filled me with joy, but now they terrified me. I didn't want to be a princess any more. Being a princess meant having the world see me... intimately. I couldn't handle that. I was barely used to being in the spotlight at all, but to date it had all been positive. That would change when the world saw the other side of me.

I forced a smile, and let George wrap his large arms around me. I felt safe again.

"Is everything okay?" George asked. "You've been a bit quiet lately."

"I thought I was quite loud actually. Especially when you started spanking me."

"You know what I mean. I can't put my finger on it, but you've not been yourself recently. Are you having second thoughts about all this?"

"No, of course not. It's just weird to hear you say I'm a beautiful princess."

"You are though. You should get used to hearing it."

"Except I'm not going to be a princess, am I? So I don't really need to get used to it."

George hugged me tighter and kissed me on the forehead. "You deserve to be a princess, and I'm going to make you one."

"You can't. And that's okay. I don't mind any more. Being a princess is probably overrated anyway. It's like what you were saying about being a prince; you don't have any say over your life and spend your entire time cutting ribbons."

"I've been thinking about that," George said slowly. "Maybe it won't be that bad. The royal family isn't as important these days, so I'll have more freedom, and I can raise tons of money for charity. It might even be enough to make a difference one day."

"That's great," I replied weakly. "So you want to be a prince?"

"I thought that's what you wanted? You thought I was crazy for giving it up."

"I know. And I'm glad you're considering it. Just promise you'll think about it before making a decision."

"I will. Speaking of being blue-blooded and all that, I have to go get a DNA test today. Why don't you hang out with your friends?"

"They're back up in York."

"Actually, they're in London, and they're going to be meeting you for lunch at the top of the Shard in an hour."

"They are?"

"Yep. Do you have the best husband or what?"

"Thank you." I kissed him on the cheek and then jumped out of bed to get showered and dressed.

Meeting the girls was just what I needed right now. My head was a mess, and I could rely on them to set me straight. Brutal honesty over an expensive lunch was just what the doctor ordered.

_*_

"I can't work out why you're so glum," Ellie said as she poured through the wine list. I knew for a fact she was just looking for the most expensive one, but I would have done the same thing.

"Yeah," Dani agreed. "It seems like you're living the dream. George wants to accept his role as a prince. I never really paid much attention to all that Kings and Queens stuff in school, but I'm pretty sure that would make you a princess. I even saw an article the other day that said you and George should already be King and Queen. Sounds good in my book."

I looked around to make sure there was no risk of our conversation being overheard. We were relatively safe. Not only had George reserved us a table, he'd also paid for every other table in the near vicinity to be taken out of commission. Other than watching out for waiters approaching, we could talk as we pleased.

149

"It's not a real marriage, remember," I reminded the girls. "We just signed a piece of paper and always planned to get divorced once the marriage was no longer necessary."

"Sounds like a real marriage to me," Dani said. "That's how my parents did it."

"You two are getting on okay though?" Ellie asked. "In all the photos, you two look like a real couple. Anyone would think you really were sleeping together."

I didn't say anything. I didn't need to. The red blush spreading across my face told the whole story.

"You dirty girl," Dani said far too loudly. "I'm so proud of you right now."

"What was it like?" Ellie asked.

"What do you mean 'what was it like?'"

"I don't know. Was it different being with a prince?"

"He didn't wear a crown while we did it. Although…"

"Spill the beans," Dani insisted.

"He was a lot… larger than any other man I've been with."

Ellie and Dani both purred with pleasure, before the waiter came and snapped them out of it.

"I'll have a chicken salad," I said to the waiter once the girls were done ordering their food and enough drink to last all day.

"Would you like the lunch version, or a large dinner plate?" the waiter asked.

"Large, please," I replied.

"Yeah, she's all about the large portions these days," Dani said, as she giggled with Ellie.

"Come on then," Ellie said. "What's the problem? He's a prince, he has a big dick, and he wants you to be his princess. I'm not about to do a charity fun-run for you at this rate."

Ellie had a point. No one would have any sympathy for me. All the public would see was some American girl who had come in and bagged herself a prince. When the pictures of me came out, some people would pretend to feel bad for me, but really they'd all be loving it. I'd be getting brought back down to Earth.

The only people I could count on for sympathy were Ellie and Dani.

"Have either of you two ever sexted with guys?" I asked.

"Well, yeah," Ellie replied. "Of course."

"I sent one a minute ago while you were ordering food," Dani said. Her phone vibrated shortly after as if to prove the point. "See."

Someone called Mike had replied with a paragraph of sexual excitement.

I want to take my fingers out of your pussy, and slide them into your mouth so you can taste your juices. Then I'm going to slide my tongue inside—

"Okay, I don't need to read any more of that. Does he know you're at lunch?"

"No, he thinks I'm naked in bed fingering myself something stupid."

"Do you want help crafting a sexy message for George?" Ellie asked.

"God no," I replied. "There's no shortage of dirty stuff in my brain. What about photos and things like that. Have you ever sent them?"

"Yeah," Ellie said. "Although I wish I hadn't. I hate knowing they're out there."

"I've never done that," Dani said.

"You haven't?" I asked in surprise. "I mean, I'm glad you didn't send one of them while we were ordering food, but I have to admit, I'm surprised."

"I'm not sending nude photos to a guy. If they want to see it, they can come and get it."

"Well I sent some," I said. "And not to George."

I told the girls how I'd sent photos to Stan and how he had a few video clips of us in compromising positions. Then I mentioned the email.

"That little sod," Ellie cursed. "I can't believe he would do that."

"Yeah, well you don't know him."

"How were you ever engaged to such a creep?" Dani asked.

"I was young. Didn't know any better. I would have married him if I didn't find out on my wedding day that he'd cheated on me with my best friend. And quite a few of my other friends as well."

"Fucking hell," Ellie cursed again. "So if George decides to formally become a prince, you'll have to pay Stan off?"

"That's about the gist of it," I said.

"Could you get the police involved?" Ellie asked.

"I guess. But I'm sure the pictures will leak if I do that."

For once the girls were silent. They had no suggestions or easy ways to get out of the problem, but at least they didn't blame me for the mess I'd gotten myself into.

"You have to tell George," Ellie said eventually. "He needs to know. This affects him almost as much as it does you, and he'll want to help."

"I was afraid you'd say that."

"You need to trust him."

It was trust that had gotten me into this problem in the first place. Trust in a fiancé who ended up betraying me.

Now I had to take that step again.

I trusted George, but he'd been acting strangely lately. I knew he cared for me, but he also cared about his sister and nephew. If I got in the way of them... well, I knew who he would put first.

The only good thing to come from my relationship with Stan was that it had forced me to move to England where I'd met George. Now I had to face the reality that I might once again be abandoned by the man I loved.

The first time had nearly broken my heart. If George abandoned me now, it might just deal the fatal blow.

Chapter Twenty-Four

GEORGE

So far, thanks to Harry's efforts, the mainstream media had given me space outside of the official public appearances, but I didn't know how long that would continue. I also knew that certain outlets were prone to taking extreme steps to get scoops, and frankly it was best not to trust any of them. That meant not using my phone for any conversation I hoped to keep private.

I picked up a pre-paid phone from a newsagent, loaded it with enough credit to make a long international call, and then dialed the number for Tabitha. She wouldn't answer, but I could leave a message and—

"Hello?"

"You're not supposed to answer calls from unknown numbers," I scolded.

"Oh give over," she replied. "I'm quite capable of hanging up if a reporter calls. Stop panicking."

How could I not panic? If anything happened to them, it would all be my fault.

"I've seen you on the television," Tabitha said. "A lot. I thought you were going to keep a low profile."

"I was." *But then I got tempted by the dark side.* "We decided to go out in public together, and then the rest just sort of… happened."

"You both look the part. I'd never know the relationship was fake. It is still fake, right?"

"The marriage is fake," I replied.

"Hmm… interesting choice of words." *I really needed to become a better liar.* "You still plan to get divorced soon?"

"At some point, yes."

How could I ever divorce Sophia? Pre-planned or not, it felt like one of the stupidest things a human could do. When you convinced a woman like Sophia to marry you—regards of the circumstances—you didn't just go and get a divorce. You clung on for dear life and rode out the wave for as long as possible.

"You're going to break her heart," Tabitha said solemnly.

"I'd never do that."

"You might not realize you're doing it, but that's what's going to happen."

"This has all been planned since—"

"I don't care about your plan, George, and neither does she. I see the way she looks at you when you two are together. She's either one hell of an actress, or she's not playing your little game."

"It's not a game," I snapped. "This is serious, and we both know it. In fact, I've been thinking about ignoring the inheritance and becoming a prince."

"What? Why?"

"I can raise a small fortune for charity as a prince, and I'm sure I can work out a way to funnel money to you and Liam for any therapy you need. In the long run, that has to be better than claiming my inheritance."

"Is Sophia okay with that?"

"Yeah, I'm sure she will be."

"So you haven't asked her?"

"She'd be a princess. Who wouldn't want that? That's what she deserves."

"Just promise me you'll check with her first, before you go storming off and making all the decisions. You've brought her into this mess. It's the least you can do."

"Okay, I promise. Now put Liam on. I haven't spoken to that little scamp in ages."

_*_

I'd hoped that organizing lunch for Sophia and her friends would cheer her up a bit, but it hadn't helped much. She'd been different these last few days; distant, as if she always had something else on her mind. I kept trying to talk to her about the future, but all I ever got in response was a series of polite nods and murmured 'okays.'

We went back to York, and Sophia decided to attend classes as normal. No doubt she'd attained some degree of celebrity status in the past week, but for every person who stared at her, two more would pretend she didn't exist. University students were far too cool for that kind of thing, or so they thought.

Miraculously, I managed to get a degree of privacy in the coffee shop on campus. Admittedly, I sat in a dark corner and hid behind my computer, but I still kept expecting reporters to burst in at any minute. If there was one thing that could be said for students, they did tend to move on quickly. It was no longer 'cool' to be obsessed over Sophia and me, so they acted like I wasn't there. That was just fine with me.

I'd been avoiding the online press as much as possible since this whole thing started, but when I finally looked at the media coverage, I realized why Sophia had been feeling a bit despondent.

There were hundreds of pictures on her online with me, but she was always referred to in a way that made her seem secondary to proceedings. The only detailed articles written about her went into exhaustive detail on her fashion choices, and the opinion pieces weren't always that kind.

No wonder she didn't want me to become a prince. The spotlight hadn't been kind to her so far, and I hadn't done anything to help.

"I always wondered how Clark Kent managed it, but apparently it's possible to be incognito in public with just a pair of glasses."

I looked up and saw Ellie standing over me with a fresh cup of coffee which she placed down in front of me.

"Thanks," I replied. "I'm going to need that. Sophia doesn't get out of class for another hour. Any idea how things have been for her today?"

"No," Ellie replied with a shrug. "But I'm sure she'll be fine."

"She's been a little down lately."

Ellie looked away awkwardly. She knew something. "I'm sure she's fine."

"It's about the pictures, isn't it?" I asked.

Ellie breathed a loud sigh of relief. "I'm so glad she told you about them. I knew you'd understand. Everyone does the sexting thing these days, and she was engaged to the guy at the time."

I nodded along, teeth gritted tightly, and the blood boiling in my veins, as Ellie kept talking about how unfair it was for women to get such a hard time for sending nude photos even though everyone did it.

Once Ellie went back to work, I finished the coffee—even though it was the last thing I needed—and patiently waited for Sophia to meet me.

She and I needed to have a little talk.

Chapter Twenty-Five

SOPHIA

I only had an hour until my next class, but as far as George was concerned, that was more than enough time to sneak back to my dorm for a "quick shag" as he would probably describe it.

From the intensity on his face, you'd think it had been a month not a day since we'd last had sex. He practically dragged me up to my room as if his life depending on being inside me.

I wasn't about to complain.

"What's this about sex pictures?" George yelled the second the door was shut.

Well that quickly put a dampener on proceedings. How did he know? He'd either been through my email or...

"Which one of them told you?"

"Ellie. It's not her fault. She thought I knew. Now tell me what the hell is going on."

For Stan's sake, I was glad he was in another country, because George looked about ready to kill someone right now. I knew he'd be mad, but I hadn't expected this.

"My ex-fiancé has pictures—and short video clips—of me. Naked. And doing... stuff."

"Jesus fucking Christ."

"He's threatening to release them and demanding money."

I wanted to cry, but I had to stay as calm as possible. One of us needed to or this would all blow out of control.

"Have you responded?" George asked.

"No, I've just ignored it. It's not a big deal."

"Not a big deal? How exactly is this not a big deal?"

"He doesn't know about your inheritance, so he's only expecting money if you become a prince, which you're not going to do."

George paced up and down the small dorm room rubbing his head with his hands and groaning loudly. He looked about ready to punch the wall, and knowing how thin they were, he'd likely go right through it.

Why was he so worked up by this? They were pictures of me not him, and if he wasn't going to become a prince...

"You're considering it, aren't you?" I asked. "You want to become a prince?"

"I could make a difference," he replied. "*We* could make a difference. Or at least, we could have done. Fucking hell, Sophia, what were you thinking?"

"What do you mean?"

"I mean, what were you doing sharing naked photos of yourself in the first place?"

"He was my *fiancé*," I replied defensively. "Why shouldn't I? Believe it or not, at the time, I hadn't planned to leave him at the altar and hook up with a fucking prince."

"This is going to mess everything up. You shouldn't have done it."

"Excuse me? What right do you have to tell me what I should and shouldn't do with my body? It's not like your moral code is perfect. You married me for an inheritance remember, so save the fucking lecture."

George clenched his fists, and kept pacing until he finally calmed down.

"You're right, I'm sorry." He wrapped his arm around me and brought me in for the hug I desperately needed. I could hear his heart still beating fast, but at least he was trying to calm down. "I didn't mean that. Send me the email and let me deal with it."

"No," I replied, keeping my head pressed against his chest. "I don't want you getting involved."

He put his hands on my shoulders and pushed me away from his chest, before looking deep into my eyes. "If you think I'm going to let someone threaten you like that and get away with it, then I guess you don't know me that well."

"And if you think I'm going to let you incriminate yourself in all this then I guess you don't know me that well either."

"It seems we're at a standoff, Mrs. Whittemore."

George smiled, but it was a smile covering layers of anxiety, and wasn't in the least bit reassuring.

"This might all go away," I said.

"You know Stan. Do you think he'll drop it?"

I paused, but then shook my head. "Only if you drop out of the limelight. I don't think he'll release them for the sake of it, because they are embarrassing for him as well."

"How so?"

"He wasn't quite so well-endowed as you, let's just leave it at that."

George grinned, and this time it looked like he meant it. You could always make a man happy by complementing his penis. I should remember that.

"But if I become a prince, he'll go ahead and leak the photos?"

I nodded. "There's a simple solution to all this."

"No," George said.

"You don't even know what I'm going to say yet."

"Yes I do. You're going to propose we get divorced now, and then I become a prince without you by my side."

"The photos won't mean a thing if I'm not your wife," I explained.

"And being a prince won't mean anything unless you're my princess."

This time I couldn't stop myself from crying. George hugged me tightly as my tears fell and were soaked up by his shirt. He was right; I'd messed everything up. Not just for him as a prince, but for us as a royal family.

If I'd never sent those photos…. I knew I hadn't done anything wrong, but that didn't mean I couldn't regret it.

"I'm going to sort this mess out," George whispered in my ear. "I promise."

"You should leave it alone," I sobbed.

"I can't," he replied. "I'm not letting him do this to you."

It was impossible to be worried while in George's arms. He gave off the scent of a man who fixed problems, and I knew he'd fix this one as well.

I just worried *how* he would fix it.

Chapter Twenty-Six

GEORGE

I had to look at the photos. I didn't want to—I *really* didn't want to—but I needed to know what we were dealing with.

It wasn't good.

Sophia certainly hadn't been shy in front of the camera. I couldn't pretend not to have received a few messages like this myself in the past, but on most of them you could only see one body part—not the face.

Stan had an entire collection of pictures and videos that left no doubt as to who the woman was.

I'd promised Sophia I'd deal with it, but there was one tiny problem with that. I had no idea how. I sent an email threatening him with legal action, but he just sent another back pointing out that by the time the case had gone through the courts it would be too late.

They might not be illegal anyway. I mean, they were his photos, so he could probably do what he wanted with them.

My preferred option was to get on the next flight to California and kick seven shades of shit out of him, but that wasn't realistic. My calendar had already been filled up with charity events, and the palace was working on scheduling an interview for me where I could announce my intention to be a prince. I barely had time to piss, let alone fly to the US.

Sophia had described Stan as sensible, in addition to being a slimy piece of shit. He wouldn't want to release the photos if he didn't have to. They wouldn't do him any favors with the ladies, and there were some less than flattering video clips showing him making faces that would forever haunt my dreams.

What had Sophia seen in this guy? How could a woman as perfect as her, be with a guy like this? All I knew was that I had to get her out of this mess; even if it meant paying him off.

I called Harry. I paid him to make me look good, and get me out of difficult situations. He knew me well enough to expect a sex scandal at some point, so a blackmail attempt wouldn't be completely unexpected.

"How can I help, George?" Harry said, as he answered the phone.

"I need to know a bit about the royal finances."

"Okay, I've been looking into that." I bet he had—probably wanted to know how much he'd get paid if he worked for me. "The short version is that you aren't going to starve and you'll always have a roof over your head."

"Yeah, I kind of gathered that. What about general spending? Do I get given access to a huge bank account?"

"It doesn't really work like that I'm afraid. All the money comes from the taxpayer—except for any funds you have from outside the family—so spending is closely monitored."

"I thought the family had an annual budget of millions of pounds."

"They do, but most of that goes on security. They aren't living the high-life for the most part I'm afraid."

Bugger me. This was not good news. Or was it? Maybe I could work this to my advantage.

"Just to be clear," I said, "there's no way I could get access to about six hundred thousand pounds without jumping through quite a few hoops?"

"Good lord, no. Not unless it was for housing or security. Why all the questions? Is there something I should know about?"

"No, everything's fine. Do you have the big interview scheduled yet?"

"It should be in three days' time," Harry replied. "I'm just waiting for final confirmation, and then I'll let you know."

"Okay, do me a favor, would you? Start spreading things in the media about how I'm considering becoming a prince to do my civic duty, even though it will mean forgoing family wealth, blah blah blah. I want the public to know that there is no money in it for me."

"That's fine. It's not like I'd be lying."

"Thanks, Harry."

If I became a prince, I couldn't pay Stan's bloody ransom demand anyway. I'd always known being a royal meant a lack of freedom, so it's not like I was surprised. It didn't matter to me. As long as I could look after Sophia and give her the life she deserved it wouldn't be a problem. I could inherit the money, give Tabitha what she needed, and then give the rest to Sophia. Simple. Then I'd be a prince and she would be a princess.

Or she'd leave.

She'd never promised to spend her life with me, and our vows wouldn't mean much given the circumstances. There was nothing stopping her from getting on the first plane back to America. She wouldn't want to hang around with the threat of those photos over her head like a sword. She'd want to leave the limelight for good, unless... unless I ended this for good.

I emailed Stan again.

I cannot and will not pay the ransom. You might think princes swim in pools of money, but that isn't the case. I won't even have control over my own bank account. Google it if you don't believe me.

That might have been a slight exaggeration, but who cared.

Look up the royal finances if you want a better idea of how it works. The only money I can spend is the money I have already. I'm happy to make a cheque out to you for £25.60 if you like.

I should have stopped and sent the email then, but I couldn't help myself.

I don't know what Sophia saw in you, but she's under my protection now. Anyone who threatens to hurt her will have to get through me first. If I see you so much as wish her a happy birthday on her Facebook page, I will decide to make a little royal visit to California for a personal introduction. You know the best thing about overseas visits? Diplomatic immunity. I can't be prosecuted for anything that happens to you. Think about that.

Did princes get diplomatic immunity? Probably not. Hopefully he wouldn't google that as well.

You had your chance with her and you blew it. Now stay out of her life.

I hit the send button then sent a text to Sophia.

I've dealt with it. You won't be hearing from Stan again.

Thank you, came the reply.

I typed out three words, but hesitated before sending the reply. I'd wanted to say them for ages, but it wasn't right to do it over a text.

I'd tell her the next time I saw her. She needed to know how I felt. Nothing about this marriage felt fake anymore, and that scared the shit out of me.

Chapter Twenty-Seven

SOPHIA

I arrived at the lecture hall ten minutes early and was one of the first to take my seat. That way I wouldn't have to deal with everyone staring at me and gossiping as I walked in.

My usual seat was still available; it was the perfect spot for me. About one third of the way up, so I was close enough to see and hear everything clearly while not being so close that I could practically count the professor's nose hairs. The back rows had always been a no-go zone. I'd never been popular enough to sit at the back when I was younger, and that attitude had kind of stuck with me.

I opened my books, and kept my head down as everyone else walked in. I didn't see the stares, but I could feel them. People were looking at me, and there was far more talk than normal for a class that started at nine in the morning.

Fortunately, if there was one group of people that didn't give a shit about celebrity gossip, it was history professors.

"Settle down, everyone," Professor Jackson yelled out. He stubbornly refused to use a microphone during class, but he seemed to enjoy the shouting. Professors like

Jackson were one of the reasons I had come to England to study. He looked a bit like a stuffy Harvard professor with the elbow patches and mismatched pants and jacket, but the messy hair and erratic way of talking gave him that 'Hogwarts professor' vibe that only a non-native could really appreciate. The locals all just took it for granted.

"I hope you all used the break constructively," Professor Jackson began. "At the very least, I hope you made it through the assigned reading." That much I had done at least. It had taken me three times as long as it should have thanks to the distraction that was George and his penis. "I've started receiving some of your essays, but there are many more still due. Make sure you have them to me by the end of the week. Now we're going to move on to the period following the execution of Charles I."

It felt so good to be back to some degree of normality. I still couldn't hear the word "prince" without thinking of George, but fortunately that word didn't come up too often. It would in future classes, and I'd have to deal with it, but for now I was safe.

Professor Jackson had steadfastly refused to let laptops into the classroom, so we all scribbled notes on paper as he spoke. I preferred writing by hand anyway—you retained more information that way.

I'd always enjoyed these classes, but I didn't want to just enjoy them any longer. I wanted to ace them. Hell, I *needed* to ace them. There was no way my grades would stay private. They'd be leaked so quickly *The Sun* would probably know them before I did. I couldn't just coast along and try to get a 2:1, but settle for a 2:2. I had to aim for a first class degree.

Mind you, even if I did well, people would just assume the grade had been bought and paid for. I was in a no-win situation. Do well and no one would believe I'd earned it. Do badly and people would think I was stupid.

Not to mention the added embarrassment of failing a class that centered on the English royal family. The irony would cause no end of amusement.

Fifteen minutes into the class, my eyelids started to feel heavy, and my head slumped forward, before snapping back as I fought off sleep. I'd packed a thermos of coffee, but I didn't usually have to dip into that until around eleven. Not today.

I poured a cup, and felt awake before even taking a sip. I wasn't the only one struggling to stay with it. My usually attentive classmates looked bored and sleepy. Heads were resting in hands, or slumped so low to the desk it was hard to tell if they were reading from the textbook of just taking a nap.

Professor Jackson deserved an attentive audience, but he was the one who insisted on teaching the first class of the morning. Rumor had it, he actually wanted the class to start at seven in the morning, so that his day would be completely finished by lunch and he could focus on his research. The university had vetoed that one; even clever students wanted to go and get drunk once in awhile.

Halfway through the lecture, something changed. There was movement and rustling behind me as people tried to subtly take phones out of pockets and bags. Professor Jackson had banned all use of phones, but those sat behind me obviously figured they could get away with it.

Once a few people had pulled out their phones, the rest of the room followed their lead. Only myself and those in front of me continued to pay any attention to the lecture. University was cheaper in England, but you still had to pay for it. I never ceased to be amazed at how little people cared about learning after spending thousands on their education.

Professor Jackson tried to carry on talking, but he couldn't ignore the commotion that was spreading throughout the room. Students weren't just using their phones; they were giggling and whispering excitedly.

I was about ready to turn to the girl behind me and ask what all the fuss was about when Ellie burst into the room loudly and out-of-breath.

"Sorry," she muttered to a bemused looking Professor Jackson. "I need to speak to Sophia. Sophia Whittemore. It's an emergency."

"Fine," Professor Jackson said, holding his hands up in defeat. "Leave quickly and quietly please, Mrs. Whittemore."

I grabbed my books and shoved them into my bag as I hurriedly left the room. Ellie looked panicked, and for a girl as calm as her, that had me worried.

"What's wrong?" I asked, the second we were outside. "Has something happened to George?"

"No, George is fine," she replied. Ellie walked so quickly I had a job to keep up with her. "I'll explain back at my dorm."

We rushed back to Ellie's room which was only a few minutes away. Students stared at us as we walked, and I could swear I saw a few of them smile. I'd gotten plenty of looks from the public recently, but there was something unnerving about those smiles.

Ellie shut the door behind us the second we were in her room. I felt like we had just escaped a pack of zombies, and half expected her to barricade the door and push all the furniture in front of it.

"What the hell is going on, Ellie? You look like you've seen a ghost."

"I wish that was all I'd seen." She opened up a message on her phone and passed it to me. "This email is doing the rounds on the university server. I haven't seen any news stories on it yet, but it's only a matter of time."

The email had a subject line of "Her Royal Highness' royal tits."

Oh fuck. Please no. Please. Anything but this.

There was no text to the emails, just some photo attachments. I opened the first one, but didn't need to open any more.

"I'm so sorry," Ellie said, wrapping her arm around me.

"Me too," I replied. "About everything."

The dream was over. There was no way I could be a princess now. I didn't know if I wanted to be.

My own phone rang. No need to guess who it was. I hit the decline button on George's call.

"You should speak to him," Ellie said. "He might be able to help."

"He promised me he'd sorted it. Just last night he said this wouldn't be a problem any more. Now look what's happened."

"I'm sure he tried."

"He should have tried harder."

I probably wasn't really mad at George, but he'd have to bear the brunt of my anger for the time being. He was a fucking prince; he should have been able to fix this. Instead, here I was, trapped in my friend's room, while pictures of my breasts circulated the university, and soon the country. Then the world.

This was only the beginning. There were plenty more photos. Stan had other photos he could release if he wanted to. And then there were the video clips.

The embarrassment wouldn't be ending any time soon.

After running from my own wedding, I hid from the world until the worst of it had blown over. How long would that take this time?

I might never see the light of day again.

Chapter Twenty-Eight

GEORGE

Sophia wasn't returning my calls, but Ellie kept me up-to-date. The two of them were holed-up in Ellie's apartment while the media ran the story continuously.

At least most of them had the sense not to show the pictures, although anyone who could use a keyboard and a search engine could find them online easily enough. The palace had engaged a small army of solicitors to shut down any site hosting the images, but they were just playing whack-a-mole and could barely keep up.

The simple fact was, anyone who wanted to look at an image of my wife's breasts could now do so. That horrified me, so I couldn't begin to imagine how Sophia felt.

She'd blame me, and she had every right to. I'd promised to solve the problem. I'd told her it had been fixed. She'd trusted me, and I'd failed her.

The pictures weren't even the end of the problem. Stan had sold his story to some hack "news" website, and according to him, Sophia had been a serial cheat who left him at the altar and broke his heart.

He'd made ten, maybe twenty, thousand—tops—from selling the story and pictures. How could he destroy someone's life for so little?

"What are our options?" I asked Harry. "There has to be something we can do."

"It's all damage control from here on out. You need to control the narrative. Get the story out there that Stan is the wrong-doer and Sophia is innocent in all this."

"That should be easy enough," I replied. "It's the truth after all."

"Are you sure?"

"Of course I'm fucking sure. He cheated on her with her best friend. Surely the public will take her word over his?"

"She doesn't look great right now."

"Because she took a few naked photos on her mobile phone with an ex? Fucking hell. He's the one that leaked them—he's the one who shouldn't have any credibility."

"I agree," Harry said. "I'm just telling you what the public is thinking right now. She's not just a random actress or pop star, George. She's going to be a princess. She might even be the Queen one day. People get funny about this kind of thing."

"Jesus Christ," I yelled as I slammed my palm against the wall in frustration. "I'm going to kill him. I'm seriously going to fucking kill him."

"I wouldn't recommend it, sir," Harry replied dryly.

"I want everyone out there speaking to the media and giving Sophia's side of the story."

"And what is that?"

"That the photos were meant to be private, and she never gave permission for them to be shared. This is a textbook case of revenge porn from a jilted ex-lover."

"Can we get her on camera?" Harry asked.

"No, I don't want those savages asking her questions."

"She should apologize. If she just says she's sorry, we can quickly move past this."

"Apologize?" I spat the word out as if it were venomous. "What the hell should she apologize for?"

"The photos were—"

"No one else's fucking business. She's not going to apologize."

Sophia would kill me if she could hear me making decisions for her like this, but she wasn't taking my calls, so what choice did I have?

"Don't forget the charity efforts," Harry said.

"What about them?" I asked, a little more calmly. It didn't do any good to take my anger out on Harry. He was a media professional—that didn't mean he agreed with half that crap that was coming out of his mouth. At least, I hoped it didn't.

"Sophia was the face of that charity drive along with you. We've already lost £100,000 in canceled donations, and new donations have all but stopped."

"Who in their right mind cancels a charitable donation because someone was the victim of a crime?"

"Rich old men," Harry replied. "They made donations because they wanted to be associated with you and Sophia. They no longer want to be associated with Sophia."

"You can bet your arse they're jerking off to the photos though."

Harry nodded. "Most likely."

I ran my fingers through my hair—might as well enjoy the experience while I still had some. If this went on for much longer, I wouldn't have any hair left.

"What do we do?" I asked quietly. I didn't have the energy for shouting any more.

"You're not going to like what I suggest."

"Just spit it out."

"You said there were more photos?"

I nodded. "Video clips as well."

"We need to get them out there."

"No fucking way. Absolutely not."

175

"We can't start damage control when we know there's another tsunami on the way."

"That is one hundred percent not going to happen. Just to be abso-*fucking*-lutely clear about this, if those images get out there, I am going to personally deal with the individual responsible. Understand?"

"I think I get the gist," Harry replied, in typically emotionless fashion. "In that case, your only option is to distance yourself from Sophia. Talk about separation and then we can sort out a divorce in a few months."

Exactly as we'd planned from the beginning. It should be easy really.

"No," I replied. "Think of something else."

"Those are the only options I can see right now. Is it really that big a deal?"

"You don't think divorcing my wife is a big deal?"

"Come on, George. Your marriage to Sophia was hardly built on a solid foundation."

"It's more complicated than that."

"Okay, but whatever you do, you need to do it quickly."

I sent Sophia a message asking her to call, but I knew it was pointless. A few blue ticks on the message told me that she'd read it, but I didn't get a reply.

"Set up an interview," I said to Harry. "With the BBC. Tell them they can ask any questions they want. Warts and all."

"You sure?"

"Yeah, let's get everything out in the open. Then we'll start damage control."

I should have listened to my gut all along. I could have claimed my inheritance, dumped the money into a trust for Liam, and then paid Stan off. I didn't like him winning, but at least that way Sophia would never have been publicly humiliated.

I closed my eyes and tried to imagine what she must be going through right now. I'd do anything to be there with her. I'd wrap my arms around her and we could pretend we were the only two people in the world.

Instead, we were two of the most famous people in the world, and the media had sunk its claws in deep. It was all my fault. I should have listened to Sophia when she recommended we stick to the original plan and ignore the royal family.

Now Sophia was royally screwed, and there was nothing I could do to help.

Except maybe one last thing.

It was all or nothing time.

Chapter Twenty-Nine

SOPHIA

"What's he saying now?" I asked.

"What is who saying?" Ellie replied, looking at her phone.

"I know you're talking to George. I saw his name pop up on your phone."

"Well you won't reply to any of his messages."

"I don't know what to say."

I didn't trust myself with my phone. If I replied to his messages, I'd take out my anger on George and I knew that wasn't a good idea. It wasn't his fault, but every time I thought about those pictures, I blamed George.

If I'd never met him, I wouldn't be in this mess. Those pictures wouldn't be out there, and I wouldn't be the laughing stock of the entire world.

But I'd still be miserable. I'd still be working in a café and destined to return home to America where I'd betrayed all my friends and family. And I'd be without George.

"He just wants to know you're okay," Ellie said. "He feels awful about all this."

"So he should. He told me it was all sorted, and suddenly my tits are all over the internet."

"It's not his fault."

"I know. I fucking know. I just… ugh, this whole thing sucks."

"Yeah, I'm with you on that one. You're welcome to stay here as long as you like, by the way."

"Thanks, but it's not like there's a lot of space in here. The last thing I need is a story about sharing a single bed with a woman to go around."

"Fair point. I do think it would be best to get back to normality as soon as possible."

I'd already tried that. I'd gone to class this morning as if I weren't married to a prince, and look how that had turned out. I wasn't destined to have a simple life. I got engaged to my childhood sweetheart and he turned out to be a cheating asshole. The next guy I meet ends up being a prince, and suddenly my tits are all over the Internet.

To think, I'd been quite boring as a teenager. I'd dreamed about having an exciting life.

What I wouldn't give to be boring now.

"George is going on television," Ellie said suddenly, staring at her phone. "It's going to be on BBC One in thirty minutes."

"Oh God," I muttered. "This is going to be bad."

"You don't know that. He's going to stick up for you."

"I don't think so. Harry will have told him he needs to distance himself from me. That's the only way he can be a prince and do some good."

"Even if he does, he won't mean it. Not in his heart."

"I don't know about that," I replied.

"Well I do. You only have to see the way he looks at you."

"That's—"

"It's not just a show for the cameras," Ellie interrupted. "And it's not just him going along with the plan. He likes you. A lot. And you like him as well."

"I guess we'll see."

"You don't have to watch it."

"Yes, I do."

"Okay, well in that case, you're going to need a cup of tea."

_*_

George looked worse than I did. He clearly hadn't let anyone put any makeup on him, judging by the bags under his eyes, and he hadn't shaved in at least two days. Harry must be sleeping on the job to let George go on the air like that.

The interview was being broadcast live, and the lack of preparation was evident. The cameras started broadcasting while George and the host were still being mic'd up. I recognized the interviewer from one of the breakfast shows—Kimberly I think. She was frantically reading through notes on a piece of paper, probably trying to memorize the questions she planned to ask.

There wouldn't be much in the way of pleasantries. This interview was interrupting planned programming which meant it was important. The BBC was about to reveal some big news about the prince and his wife. Or would that be ex-wife?

"Want another cup of tea?" Ellie asked.

"I'm still on this one."

"Well I need more. I always drink tea when I'm nervous."

After another minute or two, the interviewer finally introduced herself and her guest, and apologized for interrupting the television. It was only cricket, so I failed to believe anyone really cared.

"Good morning, Your Royal Highness," Kimberly said to George.

"Please, let's just stick to George for the time being."

"Okay, George. We'll cut to the chase as you requested. Recently sexually explicit photos of your wife

181

were leaked online. No doubt this event is proving incredibly embarrassing for the two of you, even more so considering the photos were not sent to you, but to an ex-lover. Would you care to tell us how you feel about this situation?"

My heart raced as the camera cut to George who looked surprisingly calm. Was this how I would hear about my divorce? Our entire marriage had been played out in the media, so it seemed appropriate somehow.

I didn't want to lose him, but as I looked at his face, I realized I already had. I could only hope he let me go out with some dignity.

"First of all," George began, "the leak of these photos constitutes a serious crime. The person responsible will be punished."

"That person being her ex-fiancé?"

"Yes, it would appear so."

"The leak must be a source of considerable embarrassment for you?"

"I'm not embarrassed, I'm angry."

"But how do you feel that another man has explicit photos of your wife?"

"Obviously I'd rather he didn't still have them, but my wife has a past, as do I."

"Are you annoyed with her for being so careless?" Kimberly asked.

George looked annoyed all right, but he directed his anger towards the interviewer.

"Why would I be annoyed with Sophia? She had a sex life before she met me, as did I. Frankly, I find your question to be almost as offensive as the leak of the photos."

Kimberly squirmed awkwardly in her seat, but she managed to retain a composed expression.

"Go, George," Ellie yelled. "He's taking her to task. Uptight bitch."

I smiled, but I knew George was about to drop a bombshell. If he'd just wanted to have a go at Stan, he could have released an official statement. There was more to come.

Kimberly turned a page in her notes, hopefully skipping past any other questions she might have had concerning my blame in all this. George was glaring at her so intently, I almost felt sorry for her.

"What will you do next?" Kimberly asked. "The photos are out there and they're all anyone is talking about. Like it or not, this is going to affect your position as a prince and Sophia's as a princess."

"You're right," George admitted. "This will die down eventually, but in the meantime the news has already had a huge impact on my fundraising efforts. That's pathetic, by the way, but unfortunately it's true."

I groaned loudly in frustration. "Great, so now I've taken money from charities."

"No, Stan has," Ellie replied. "You cannot blame yourself over this. I know I sound like a broken record, but it's true."

"We're going to have to get divorced," I said, with a heavy heart. "That's the only solution."

"George will find a way," Ellie said. "He has to."

"So that's the plan?" Kimberly asked George. "You're just going to wait for this all to die down?"

"Sort of. The problem is it could drag on for a long time. Especially if more photos get released."

Oh shit.

"There are more photos?" Kimberly asked.

"What's he doing?" I asked Ellie helplessly.

"I... I don't know."

"There are more," George admitted. "As I said, I want this to die down as quickly as possible."

"Please don't do this," I said to the televised version of George as I realized what he was about to do.

183

"There are more photos," George said. "And I'm going to release them now. We want to take control of the situation."

"I'm sure he's not actually going to—" Ellie stopped in her tracks as George pulled his phone out of his pocket.

"I can't watch," I said, as I kept watching anyway.

I wanted to look away, but this was my brain's way of punishing myself. George was about to show the world everything. My breasts were already online, but soon there would be full nude images, as well as videos of me masturbating, and even one with cum on my face. A woman pictured with cum dripping down her cheeks could never become Queen.

"I know it's pre-watershed," George said, "but I'm sure your viewers can look away."

"I don't think we can—" Kimberly began. She stopped arguing as she looked off-camera and presumably got the nod from her boss. "Apparently we can."

"I'll cut to the chase," George flicked through a few screens on his phone. "This is the worst one. A full, close up shot of the genitals. Personally, I think it's a beautiful picture, but the public will be the judge of that."

He's doing it. He's actually fucking doing it. He's going to show my pussy to the entire world.

"Is it a good picture, at least?" Ellie asked.

I knew she was trying to lighten the mood, but I wasn't interested. Harry must have convinced George this was the right thing to do, but he was screwing me over in the process.

George held his phone up to the camera which slowly zoomed in and then focused on the image on his screen.

"Oh. My. God," Ellie said loudly. "That is lush."

"It's… It's…."

"It's huge," Ellie said. "Bloody hell, Sophia. You told me he was big, but that's ridiculous."

I heard Kimberly gasp off camera as she saw the image on the phone. And what an image it was.

I stared at the rock hard, nine-inch cock I knew and loved. So did the rest of the world.

"That's one of the more flattering photos," George said. "There are some where I'm more… relaxed, and one where—I swear to God—it was really cold when I took the photo."

"That's your…" Kimberly began. "These are your photos?"

"Yep. They're ones I've sent to ladies in the past. They'd probably come out sooner or later. Loads of people do it these days, and I don't see why women should be the only ones publicly shamed about it."

George put his phone away, and waited for Kimberly to ask him another question. She looked suitably speechless. The camera lingered on her for ten seconds until she suddenly snapped into life, presumably after receiving a word in her ear.

"We should probably go back to the cricket briefly," Kimberly announced. "Just to gather our thoughts."

"I have one more announcement," George said. "But it can wait."

As was her habit, Ellie turned the television off the second the cricket appeared on the screen. "Well, that was interesting."

"Yeah," I replied. "Interesting."

"You're still here."

"I should probably—"

"Go screw that massive cock that women all over the world are fantasizing about right now? Yeah, you should probably go do that."

I smiled and grabbed my things. Everyone would still be talking about me, but I didn't care anymore. I had George.

He had one more announcement to make, and if it was half as interesting as the last one, I wanted to be there when he made it.

Chapter Thirty

GEORGE

You had to be cold-blooded to give interviews on television. The bright lights had me sweating heavily and that was without the layer of makeup someone had tried to plaster on my face before I came out here.

It probably didn't help that I'd come on television specifically with the goal of showing my erect penis to the public. That was bound to cause the odd bit of anxiety.

And that hadn't even been the big news of the day.

"Do you want me to ask you any particular questions?" Kimberly asked during the break. The cricket was probably getting its best viewing figures in years. "If you like, I can just let you read a speech. It sounds like you have something you want to get off your chest."

"I do," I replied. "I'll just make a short statement. It won't take long. Then you can all go back to talking about me. Trust me, there's going to be a lot to talk about."

"We're going to wait half an hour," Kimberly said. "The execs want to let word spread online about the interview for maximum viewing figures."

"I understand."

I pulled out my phone and eagerly looked for a message from Sophia. Nothing. I'd taken a big risk, and I was about to take an even bigger one. I wanted her by my side, but as far as she knew, I'd betrayed her trust. Given time, I might be able to earn that back, but I wasn't sure I'd get that time. I wasn't sure I deserved it.

Ellie wasn't responding to messages either, which meant she was likely comforting Sophia. The second all this was over, I'd go to her and apologize. I'd get down on my knees if I had to. Whatever it took.

I tried to stay offline, but boredom and a smartphone made that impossible. News sites were struggling to keep up, and as always, Twitter was way ahead of proceedings. My cock had already been hashtagged as #royalschlong, and I was being referred to as 'George IX' in honor of my greatest asset.

The plan had worked. No one was talking about Sophia's breasts any more. Boobs were everywhere you looked, but erect penises were not often flashed about outside of porn sites. One particularly on-the-ball website was already crowdfunding to produce dildos based on a mold of my penis. I didn't know how to feel about that, but for the time being I decided to treat it as flattering.

"Okay, we're back on in sixty seconds," a producer yelled.

A second later, I heard a familiar voice in the crowd of journalists, cameramen, assistants, producers, and pretty much every other BBC employee who happened to be in the building at the time.

"I want to speak to him," I heard Sophia say. I looked around but couldn't see her.

"Thirty seconds," the producer yelled.

Screw this, I needed to talk to her before I went on air. I wouldn't be able to explain, but at least she would know how I felt.

I leapt out of my chair, and ran towards the sound of her voice. She'd been through hell the last few hours, and yet she still looked dazzling. She still looked like a princess.

"Twenty seconds."

"Hey," I said, as we both stood face-to-face for the first time in what felt like months.

"Hey."

"I'm so glad you came. There's no time to explain, but you're going to hear some bad things."

"Ten seconds."

"I just need you to remember that I love you, okay?"

Sophia smiled and nodded. She trusted me. Somehow, after everything I'd done, she still trusted me.

"Five seconds."

I jogged back to the chair and sat down just as we went live. Kimberly spoke for a few moments, and then passed over to me.

Here goes nothing.

"Thank you Kimberly." I took a deep breath. The entire country would soon hate me, but there was only one person's affection I still cared about. Unfortunately, she might hate me too. "I have been living a lie, and have been ever since the news of my parenthood became public knowledge."

I pictured families sat around glued to their television sets, until I remembered that families didn't do that anymore. The parents might be watching television, but the kids would be in the same room bashing information into Twitter as fast as their thumbs could move.

What will be the hashtag for this one, I wonder?

"More accurately," I continued, "Sophia and I have been living a lie. Our marriage was a fraud."

I didn't have to imagine the gasps of shock around the country, because everyone behind the camera did exactly that.

189

"I needed to be married to claim an inheritance left in my mother's will, so I convinced Sophia to marry me as a favor. Sophia had nothing to gain from all this, and as you have seen, everything to lose. She's the innocent victim here."

Good job we never filed that visa application.

The only people who knew that I'd promised Sophia financial reward were Ellie and Dani, and I knew I could rely on them to keep the secret.

I looked for Sophia in the crowd, but I couldn't see her through all the bright lights shining into my eyes. It was probably for the best; I didn't want to see the look on her face when I said the next bit.

"Sophia and I care for each other a great deal, but due to the circumstances surrounding our marriage, we shall be immediately seeking a divorce or annulment."

I just need you to remember that I love you, okay?

"I never wanted to be a prince, but the reaction from the public completely blew my mind. Unfortunately, as a famous man once said, 'with great power comes great responsibility.' It turns out that I'm not capable of taking on that responsibility. Sophia would have made a great princess—and she is a princess in my eyes—but I am not fit to be a prince. Therefore, I am officially abdicating and renouncing any claim I may have to the throne. Thank you ladies and gentleman, that will be all."

I stood up and walked off the set to stunned silence. Royal analysts would have a field day over the coming days and weeks trying to figure out what the hell was going on, but right now I only wanted to hear from one person.

I didn't need to find Sophia; she found me.

"So, we're getting divorced?" she asked softly.

I nodded. "I think it's for the best. I want to start from scratch. What about you?"

"I'd rather not."

"Oh."

"I'm fine with the divorce part," she said, "but I don't want to start from scratch. Otherwise we've got to do the whole dating thing again, and that's tiresome." Sophia smiled, which meant I smiled as well, because how could I not.

"You're really okay with all this?" I asked.

"I never wanted to be a princess anyway. I thought I did, but I'd rather live a normal life. A relatively normal life anyway."

"You're still a princess to me, and as long as we're together, I'll always treat you as one."

"Not always, I hope," Sophia replied. She bit her bottom lip, and placed her hands gently on my side.

"Always," I insisted.

"I don't think you get what I'm saying." She went up on tiptoes and whispered in my ear.

"Oh, right. Yeah, good point. I won't *always* treat you like a princess. Speaking of which, I'm suddenly quite keen to get away from all these cameras. No need to give the media any more explicit photos."

"I can't believe you showed the world your cock," Sophia said, as we walked away.

"You mad?"

"No," she replied. "Seeing it is one thing, but I'm the only one who gets to sit on it. Now come on, let's get out of here."

Chapter Thirty-One

SOPHIA

George had looked exhausted from the little show he'd put on for the cameras, but the second we were in our hotel room he came back to life.

More than that. He looked more alive than I'd ever seen him. When we'd met, George had been stressed about his inheritance, and I'd been stressed out about my visa. Now neither of us had those worries. We were both free to do whatever we wanted. Fortunately, we both wanted the same thing. We usually did.

"Want some champagne to celebrate?" George asked.

"No thank you. I'd like some dick to celebrate."

George laughed out loud. "And here I am trying to be romantic."

"There's a time and place. Sex now, romance later."

George grabbed me by the wrist and pulled me into him. I immediately started undoing his pants while one of his hands cupped my face, and the other squeezed my breast firmly. My hand found his glorious member, which quickly became rock solid as I squeezed it in my palm and stroked slowly.

I had to get him in my mouth. It wasn't something I wanted to do because it felt right, or because it was 'his turn,' I just physically needed to take this solid cock into my mouth. I pulled my lips from George's and dropped to my knees. His gasp of disappointment at having my breast removed from his hand, quickly turned into a moan of pleasure, as I opened wide and took him between my lips.

The vein pulsed against my tongue, as I pressed my lips against his smooth skin and worked my way down the shaft. I'd given up trying to get the entire thing in my mouth, but I could more than make up for that by sucking it hard, ignoring the noise I made and the trail of saliva I left over his cock.

His fingers wove their way into my hair, but instead of pushing my head further down his member, he pulled me away. My lips were clasped on tightly and made a "popping" noise as he pulled me off, leaving his cock glistening and rock hard.

"No more," George said. "I'm already on the edge, and I haven't even started with you yet."

He grabbed my wrists again and lifted me back to my feet, before scooping me up into his arms and carrying me over to the bed. Sometimes I forgot just how strong George was. He'd always been dominant but gentle at the same time, never pushing the unspoken limits we both had in our minds.

I dropped down on the firm mattress and watched as George peeled off his clothes until he was completely naked.

"Your turn," he ordered.

"Why don't you come and take them off me?"

"No," he replied firmly. "I'm going to watch."

Then I'm going to take my sweet time about it.

I opened my blouse button by button, slower than I had ever done since getting changed in the locker room at school when surrounded by girls who'd blossomed far earlier than me. At least this time I was enjoying it.

I threw the blouse to one side, and unzipped my skirt before sliding it down my legs and kicking it off. George's eyes flicked between my heaving breasts, trapped in my bra, and my damp panties, just waiting to be peeled off.

"You're taking your time," George said through heavy breaths.

"I'm just giving you a longer show. More *bang* for your buck."

I was also driving myself crazy. I freed my breasts and threw my bra at George. By the time he had pulled it off his face, my panties were flying at him as well. I made a 'come here' motion with my finger, and George bounded forward, practically jumping onto the bed.

My legs opened as he slid between them, his hard cock pressing temptingly up against my belly.

"Shit, forgot the condom," George muttered. He lifted himself back up to his knees, but I hooked my legs behind him and held him firmly in place. I really didn't want to see that glorious cock covered up.

"I'm on the pill," I said softly. "And we are still married…"

"God, I was hoping you'd say that."

George came back down, but this time his mouth went straight to my nipples, covering one, and then the other, in kisses and gentle bites.

"George," I moaned, as his teeth clamped down and pulled my nipple away from my chest. Deep inside, I was vaguely aware that the sensation shooting through my body should be pain, but all I felt was pleasure. The harder he bit, the harder he pulled, the wetter I got between my legs until I was in real danger of leaving a puddle on the mattress.

"You shouldn't have kept me waiting," he growled.

His cock—still damp from where I'd sucked him—brushed against the inside of my thigh while he devoured my nipples. It was just inches from my entrance. I had to have him. My body craved him, like it craved chocolate after a session at the gym. I burned for him. He had to get inside me.

George's lips finally left my breasts, and instead he started kissing my belly, heading down towards the slick juices between my thighs.

"No," I moaned. I reached out for his hair and grabbed him just as he had grabbed me earlier when he pulled my mouth from his cock. "No more."

"I want to taste you."

"Tough. I need you to fuck me. Now."

"You're a demanding woman." George raised himself onto his knees and lifted my legs up into the air. His cock stood upright between my legs; agonizingly close to completing me.

He looked me in the eyes as his hand angled his cock down and placed it against my wet sex. The tip came agonizingly close to entering, but I still didn't have him inside me.

"You want this as much as I do," I pleaded. "Fuck me, George. I want you to slide that cock inside me and screw me until you empty your balls into my pussy."

His eyes never left mine as he slowly pushed forward and buried himself inside me. My thighs doubled back against my chest as he leaned in to kiss me firmly on the lips. I gripped the sheets and gave myself over to him completely. I knew I was in good hands.

George moved faster, with each thrust seemingly going deeper and deeper inside me. His groin pressed against my clit as he moved, building up the pressure with each stroke. Sooner or later, I would explode.

"Don't stop," I moaned. I gripped the bedsheet tighter, my body channeling the pleasure from my pussy and sending it to the very tips of my fingers.

"You have the tightest, wettest pussy I've ever fucked," George replied. "I'm not stopping until I've filled it up."

I cried out in ecstasy as I remembered he would soon be emptying his seed inside me. "Faster," I commanded. "Harder."

His cock throbbed, as he banged into me again and again, harder each time. I tightened around him, my legs pushing back against his shoulders, as if I were trying to push him away. That was the last thing I wanted; I just had no control over my body.

"I'm going to come, baby," George moaned. "I'm going to fill that tight little snatch with my cum."

I felt it. I felt him emptying himself into me as every other sense in my body disappeared in a wave of pleasure and release.

George let go of my legs and lay down on top of me as we both let out a last few shakes of bliss. He kissed my neck, but left his cock inside me, until eventually it softened and he pulled it out.

A trail of his essence left me with it, dribbling down the inside of the thigh and adding to the wet patch that had been there from the moment I'd taken off my panties.

We lay there wordlessly, until George's cock started twitching again.

"This time, I want oral," I joked.

"So do I."

George grabbed my ass and lifted it onto his face, while I spun round and bent over to get up close and personal with his cock. It was still covered in a mixture of his cum and mine. I couldn't wait to taste it.

Chapter Thirty-Two

GEORGE

"Can we afford an executive box?" Sophia asked. "This all seems rather extravagant, given our financial situation now."

"Our financial situation has changed," I replied, "but I'll tell you about that later. We're not paying for anything today. It's all free hospitality."

"Why are people paying for us to come to watch a rugby match?"

"Stop complaining, Sophia," Ellie huffed. "We get to spend the day admiring big, muscular men in tight shorts. I'd have paid a lot of money to be here."

"Yeah," Dani agreed. "This isn't cricket, after all. Now that, you'd have to pay me for."

By the end of the day, I'd likely regret inviting Ellie and Dani along with us, but Sophia always seemed happier when they were around, and I'd do anything to keep a smile on her face. The girls kept her grounded, and helped her forget she was a celebrity of sorts, even with all the special treatment we were getting today.

"We still attract attention," I explained. "The club looks good with us in the crowd, so it's a win-win situation. Except for the fact that I have to watch a West London game."

A security guard escorted us up to a corporate box just as the match was starting. Rugby was very much a secondary passion after football, but I did have a weakness for Harlequins, who just happened to be rivals with West London.

Once we all had drinks in hand, Ellie and Dani disappeared outside and took a seat in the stands—anything to get closer to the men, I suppose.

"We can go outside too, if you like," I suggested.

"Let's stay here for a bit. You can explain the rules to me, so I don't sound like an ignorant American out in the crowd. Is there an offside rule in rugby like there is in soccer?"

"Sort of."

"Shit. I hate that one."

Sophia stripped off her coat and scarf, revealing her slender curves under a tight jumper. Maybe I should have arranged for a little more privacy. How long had it been since we'd had sex? I checked my watch: about three hours. I'd started cooking some lunch, which apparently Sophia found sexy as all hell, so we got down and dirty, while the eggs remained unwhisked and the toast burned.

"Are you nervous about being in the public eye again?" I asked. "I know it's a big step coming out again like this."

"We have to do it at some point," Sophia replied. "Everyone must be so confused seeing us together after you publicly declared our divorce. You wouldn't believe the conversation I had with my mom."

"I overheard some of it. You were trying to explain why we were more in love than ever, but getting divorced anyway. I guess it does sound a little crazy."

"It was the right thing to do."

Sophia rubbed the spot on her ring finger where the engagement and wedding rings had both taken pride of place until a week ago. I'd suggested putting them in a drawer in case we ever needed them again, but Sophia had insisted on selling them. She'd been right; the rings made a small fortune in a charity auction. Far more than I paid for them in the first place. It seemed unusual that a metal band could increase in value just by spending time on Sophia's finger, but then I decided that actually made perfect sense. Sophia improved anything she touched, and that included me.

"Is this a big game?" Sophia asked. "The crowd seems up for it."

"There's nothing special about the game," I replied. "But one of the players, Oliver Cornish, is kind of a hero. This is his first game since almost single-handedly winning England the World Cup. Even the opposition fans respect him, and that's saying something."

I tried to watch the game from the comfort of our soft leather seats, but my eyes kept turning back to Sophia. She looked adorable as she tried to process what was happening on the pitch in front of her.

"Why aren't they passing it forward?" Sophia asked. "There's loads of space behind the opposition line. Someone could run through and pick up a pass."

"You can't pass it forward. It's against the rules."

"It's against the rules to pass it forward?" Sophia asked incredulously.

"Yep."

"Is that a rule in soccer as well, because it would explain a lot about why English sports are boring as hell."

"I really need to take you to a football game. That's a real sport, but rugby's cool too. It's like American football without the body armor. Ellie and Dani seem to like it."

"We both know why they're enjoying it."

With impeccable timing, Ellie and Dani both wolf whistled as Oliver Cornish approached the line for a throw. I'd expected him to retire after the World Cup, but some players just had that natural hunger in them; a fire that wouldn't go away. Oliver looked up for it today; I just wished he weren't playing for West London.

A waitress came over and offered us another glass of wine, but Sophia and I both needed caffeine after a few too many last night. For me, that meant a cup of tea. For Sophia, it was coffee.

"It'll be me serving the coffee again on Monday," Sophia said, once she had her hands around a hot mug.

"You don't have to go back to work."

"I want to. Besides, we need the money. No more playboy lifestyle for you either."

"I don't want to be a playboy anymore. However—"

"However?" Sophia asked with raised eyebrows. "You'd better not be going back to sleeping around my college again."

"I'm not sure there are many left," I replied with a grin. "But that's not what I meant. Remember I said our financial situation has changed?"

"Yeah. What did you mean by that?"

"I'm collecting the inheritance."

"What? How?"

"I got that palace solicitor to look into the trust. Turns the trust has very specific language about me marrying a woman."

"We knew that already."

"The solicitor—being a typical smartarse—pointed out that if I were gay, the clause requiring me to marry a woman would be unconscionable."

"Please God don't tell me you're planning to fake a marriage to a guy this time?"

"I was a little worried that's where the solicitor was going, but he said we could challenge the clause without me actually proving I'm gay. The trustee backed down instantly. No one wants to be the guy upholding a discriminatory clause, so he declared it invalid. The money's mine."

"Oh. Shit."

"Yeah. Still want to go back to serving coffee?"

"Maybe not."

We sat there holding hands in silence, until Sophia finally decided she wanted to get out from behind the glass and watch the game with the fans.

"They'll spot us in the crowd," I warned. "It might take five minutes, but I guarantee you they will spot us."

"So what if they do? My boobs are already on the internet for all to see. A bit of banter from the crowd shouldn't be a huge problem."

It didn't take five minutes. The second we stepped outside, the fans nearby turned around to look at us and that reaction spread throughout the ground like a Mexican wave.

Then came the chanting.

"What are they singing?" Sophia asked.

I looked over at Ellie and Dani, who were both trying hard not to laugh. "They are imploring you to show your chest," I replied tactfully.

"Get your tits out for the lads," the crowd chanted. "Get your tits out, get your tits out, get your tits out for the lads."

"Oh," Sophia said. "I hear them now."

"We can go back inside if you like?" I offered.

We both knew Sophia was going to be the subject of gossip and rude gestures for a while yet, but this was definitely a baptism of fire.

"No, it's okay," Sophia replied. "Could be worse."

Ellie and Dani leaned over to offer their support and the girls all started laughing and joking. Perhaps it had been a good idea to bring them along. The three of them stood up in unison, in the way women did when they all planned to go to the toilet together.

I turned my legs to the side to let them past, but they didn't move.

"On three," Ellie said loudly. "One. Two. Three."

The three of them—perfectly in sync—all lifted up their jumpers and bras, flashing their breasts to the crowd. I quickly looked away before I got accused of looking at more than just Sophia's, but I was the only one in the ground who did.

Tens of thousands of men all wolf-whistled in unison as the girls waved their tits around for five seconds that seemed to last an eternity.

Eventually, they all sat down and carried on watching the game as if nothing had happened. I stared at Sophia, my eyebrows having taken up permanent residency at the top of my head.

"What?" she asked innocently. "It's not like they haven't seen mine before. And fuck it, they're only boobs."

"They're not *only boobs*. They're the best boobs I've ever had my hands on. Speaking of which, I know we promised to have dinner with the girls but do you think we could—"

"Take a detour via the hotel? Yeah, I think we could swing that. I like to work up an appetite before eating."

Epilogue

SIX MONTHS LATER

SOPHIA

"What are you going to do with your last week in England?" Ellie asked.

"We don't have any plans," I replied.

"Gotcha," Ellie replied with a smile. She'd correctly deciphered the code for 'we plan to stay in bed all day and screw.'

I'd been excitedly counting down the days to my final day at work, but now that it had arrived, I couldn't help but feel a tinge of sadness. Serving coffee wasn't the most glamorous of jobs, but working with Ellie had been fun, and I'd met so many cool people here, including George.

No one gossiped about me any more—at least not in here. In the first few weeks after George's big announcement, the coffee shop had been noticeably more full than usual, and there had been plenty of gawking. That died down quickly, and now people didn't even look up when I served them their drinks. Just how I liked it.

"Soy latte for Chris," I yelled out, as I placed the coffee down on the counter. I'd finally gotten the hang of doing some very basic shapes in the foam, so at least I could say I'd learned something from this experience.

"I still can't believe you're working here," Ellie said after serving another customer. "You don't need the money."

"It keeps me grounded," I replied. "And I get to hang out with you of course."

"That's sweet, but if I were in your shoes, the only thing you'd see of me is Facebook pictures from the beach of whatever Caribbean island I happen to be on that week."

"We have plenty of time for all that. I came here to get a master's degree, and not end up in a tonne of debt. I don't want to go back to America without that."

"Why?"

I shrugged my shoulders. "I don't know. A sense of accomplishment? A feeling that I'm not a total failure?"

"You just want to say 'I told you so' to your mother."

"Yep, that's about the gist of it."

"You're going to come back to England though, right?"

"Definitely," I replied.

George and I had discussed living in America for a bit, but I struggled to find the enthusiasm to move back home. Old friends had crawled out of the woodwork during my time in the spotlight, but their two-dimensional attempts to reconnect just made me realize how little I needed them. These were the same people who'd known about Stan sleeping with my best friend, and they may have even slept with Stan as well for all I knew.

My real friends were here, and I didn't intend to leave them behind for very long. I'd have to figure out the visa situation, but I'd find a way. We'd find a way.

"I wouldn't mind if you stayed in California for a while," Ellie said.

"You wouldn't?"

"No. I've always wanted to visit, but I can barely afford the flights, let alone the accommodation."

"Glad to know I can come in use," I replied.

"I know American women like British accents on men, but do you think American men will like a woman with an English accent?"

"They won't know what your accent is. The first time we spoke, I only understood about fifty percent of the words you used."

"Oh. Guess I'd better start learning the Queen's English."

"Don't worry, you'll do just fine as you are. All men understand the language of big, bouncy boobs, and a beautiful smile."

"Glad to hear it. I wouldn't mind spending a few weeks screwing all those hot surfers I see on television."

"I'm from Northern California. We don't have hot surfers, we have pretentious hipsters."

"Well… you should move."

"You're probably right," I said with a smile.

I knew where I wanted to live, and it wasn't California. It was right here in Yorkshire. It might not be the most metropolitan part of the country, but I'd already decided that London wasn't for me.

George and I stayed in London for a month after the announcement and we were treated like royalty the entire time. We could go where we wanted, when we wanted. Sports stadiums and concert venues opened their doors to us, and we drank at so many exclusive clubs and bars that I eventually got bored of meeting celebrities. Ellie would never forgive me if she knew I'd turned down the chance to meet Lady Gaga because I'd wanted an early night. George was just as bad. I'd wanted to go to a club to meet Jennifer Lawrence, but George had insisted we go back to the hotel instead.

The special treatment quickly grew tiresome. We didn't deserve it. We were just two people who had fallen in love. That was more than enough for me.

I'd told George that I wanted to finish my degree, so we'd come back to Yorkshire, and immediately I felt at home again. We got our fair share of curious glances, but if we wanted to get into a club we had to stand in line like everyone else. I loved it.

Even the accent had grown on me, and you couldn't beat being referred to as "pet." It was like being welcomed into the family. Not that I could use the word myself. I'd said it once to a customer, but he just looked at me with a bemused expression on his face.

"I hope we're still on for drinks tonight?" Ellie asked.

"Sure. I'm not the one who has to work tomorrow. How about going back to Viva? Seems an appropriate place given how eventful our last visit was."

Ellie laughed. "Yeah, I'm up for that. Today is all about the déjà vu it seems."

"What do you mean?"

"Never mind. Can George make it?"

"He goes where I tell him," I joked. "Speak of the devil."

George walked through the doors of the café looking surprisingly overdressed for a hot spring day. Not that I was complaining. No one could pull off the suit look quite like George. He'd forsaken the tie, and had a few shirt buttons undone, which probably went some way to explaining why I liked the look so much.

"Hi, George the Ninth," Ellie said loudly.

The nickname had stuck, and no one took more pleasure in using it in public than Ellie. She even wrote "George IX" on this cup whenever he came in for a drink. George had tried referring to Ellie as "Ellie 34D" but it didn't have quite the same ring to it. Not to mention, he got her size completely wrong.

"Hi, Ellie," George replied quietly.

"Everything okay?" I asked. George didn't have his usual confidence or swagger about him today, and he'd been cryptic about what he'd been up to the last few days. I hadn't been worried about it—until now.

"I'm not sure yet," George replied.

"How did your meeting go?"

"I got what I needed."

George looked behind me to Ellie, and then back to me. He had bad news. We were set for money, so it wasn't that. Could he not come to America with me anymore?

"Sophia, would you go collect those cups from that empty table?" Ellie asked.

"You're going to miss bossing me around when I'm gone."

"Stop complaining and go get the cups, love."

"She's only this annoying when you're here," I said to George, as I went around the counter towards the empty table.

"That's my fault," George said. "She's doing me a favor."

I walked towards the table, but George blocked my way. Ellie mentioned déjà vu earlier, and suddenly I knew what she meant.

George dropped to one knee in front of me and took hold of my left hand. "We didn't do it properly last time and that was my fault. This time I want it to be perfect. You're my princess and always will be. You deserve to get married like one."

He pulled out a small box from the inside of his jacket pocket and opened it in front of me.

"Sophia Simpkins, will you marry me?"

I didn't look down at the ring. I didn't need to. The size of the rock didn't matter. All that I cared about was the love and affection I saw in his eyes. I knew I wanted to wake up to that look every day for the rest of my life.

My mouth couldn't even form the one-syllable word response, so I just nodded my head frantically until George stood and lifted me up in his arms. I was vaguely aware of some clapping and cheering in the background, but all I could see through tear-filled eyes was Ellie wiping her own tears from her cheeks.

My last maid of honor had betrayed me. This time, I knew I'd be in safe hands. I had the perfect man and the perfect friends.

Life couldn't get any better.

"We're going to do it right this time," George whispered in my ear.

"I don't care how we do it," I replied. "I just want to be with you."

"I've already booked the honeymoon."

"Where are we going?"

"I'd love to spend two weeks looking at you in a bikini," George replied. "But I made a promise to you and I'm a man of my word. We're going skiing."

THE END

About the Author

Jessica Ashe is a twenty-seven year old British woman currently enjoying the much nicer weather found in Northern California. She enjoys writing about sophisticated and intelligent women and the hot alpha males that lust after them.

You can contact Jessica at author.jessicaashe@gmail.com, follow her on Twitter at @AsheRomance, and on Facebook.

Made in the USA
Las Vegas, NV
06 November 2024

11208313R00125